W9-CHV-470

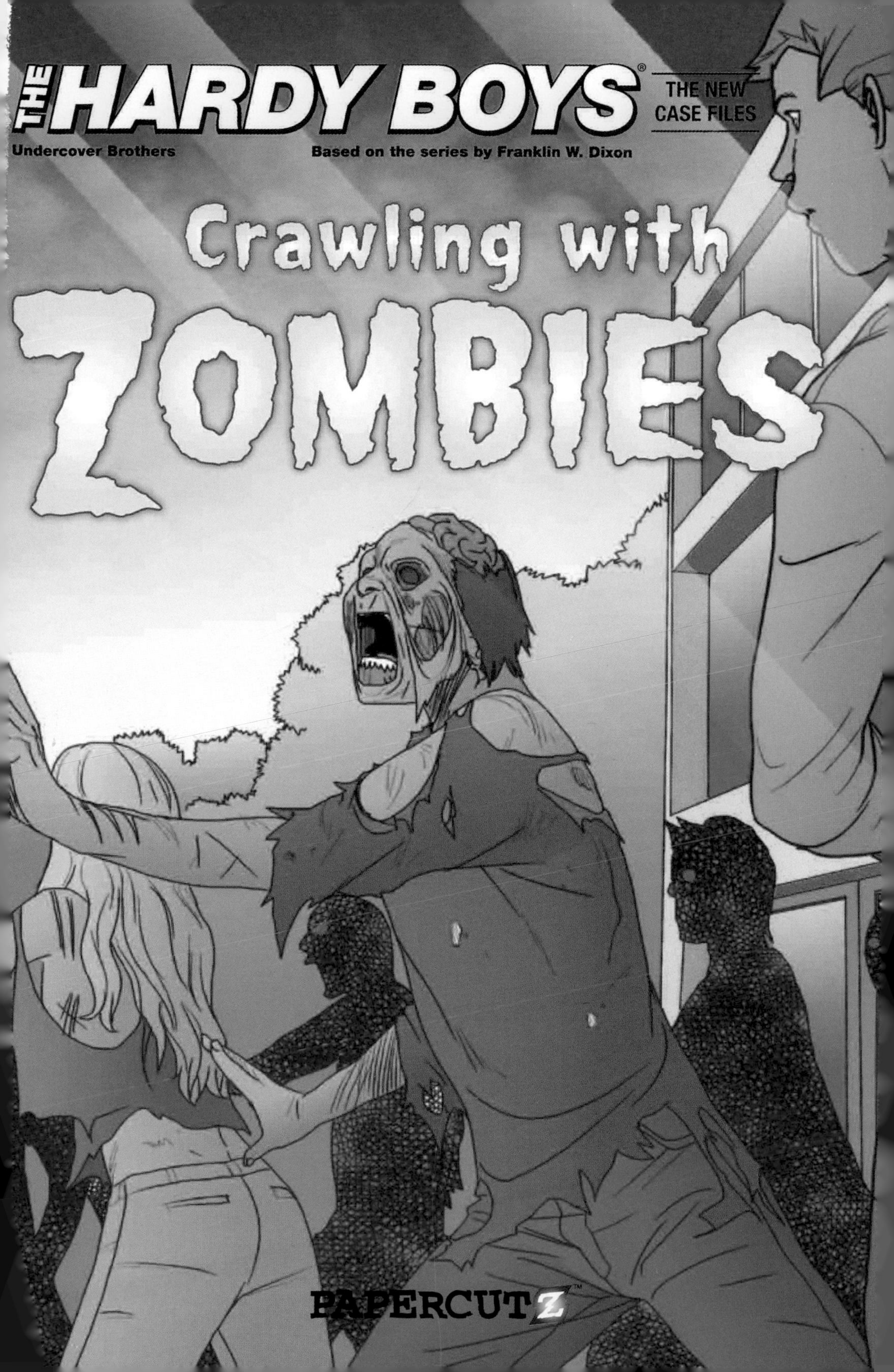
THE HARDY BOYS®
THE NEW CASE FILES
Undercover Brothers
Based on the series by Franklin W. Dixon
Crawling with ZOMBIES
PAPERCUTZ™

THE HARDY BOYS GRAPHIC NOVELS FROM PAPERCUTZ

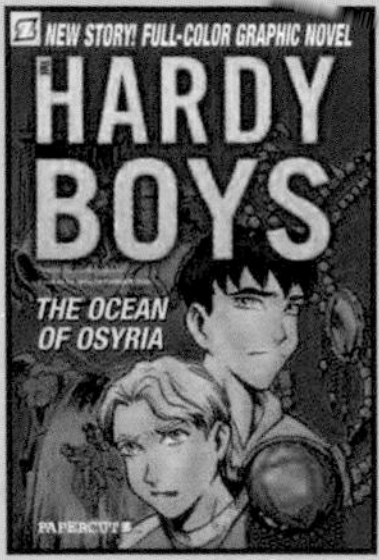
NEW STORY! FULL-COLOR GRAPHIC NOVEL
HARDY BOYS
THE OCEAN OF OSYRIA
PAPERCUTZ

#1 "The Ocean of Osyria"

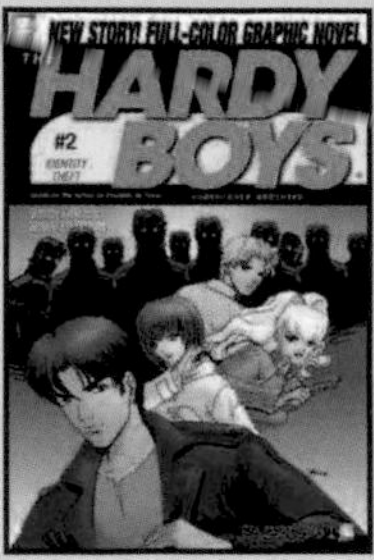
NEW STORY! FULL-COLOR GRAPHIC NOVEL
HARDY BOYS
#2

#2 "Identity Theft"

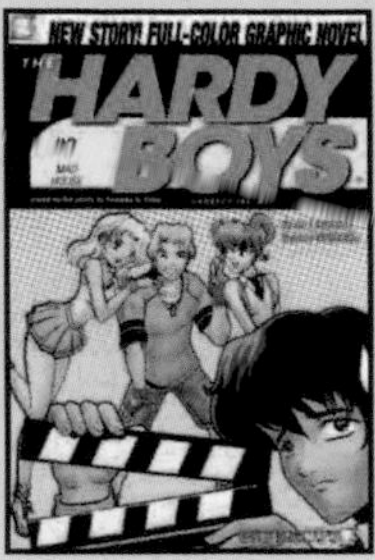
NEW STORY! FULL-COLOR GRAPHIC NOVEL
HARDY BOYS

#3 "Mad House"

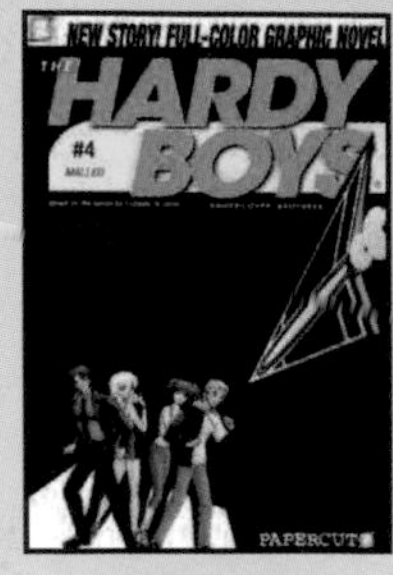
NEW STORY! FULL-COLOR GRAPHIC NOVEL
HARDY BOYS
#4
PAPERCUTZ

#4 "Malled"

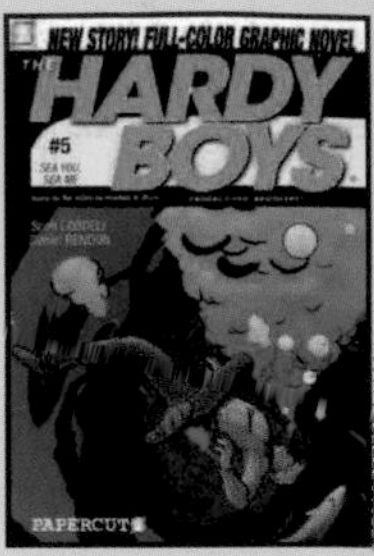
NEW STORY! FULL-COLOR GRAPHIC NOVEL
HARDY BOYS
#5
PAPERCUTZ

#5 "Sea You, Sea Me!"

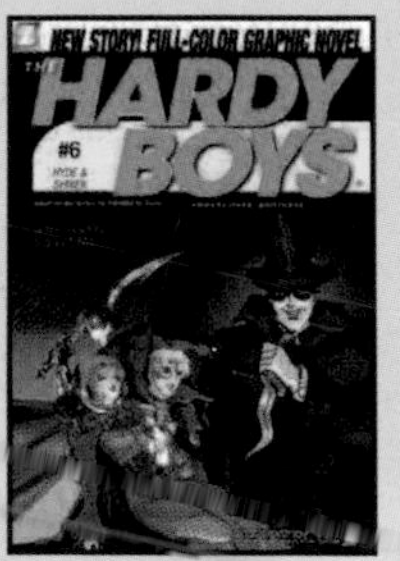
NEW STORY! FULL-COLOR GRAPHIC NOVEL
HARDY BOYS
#6

#6 "Hyde & Shriek"

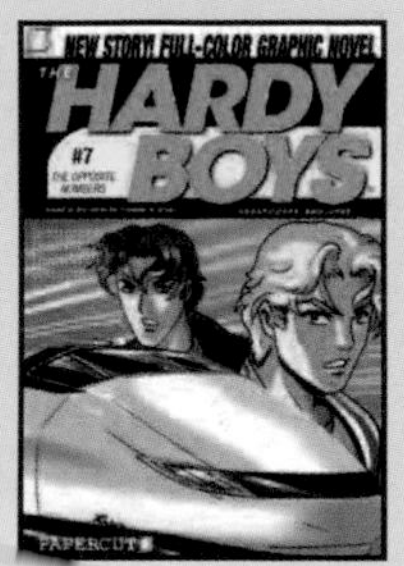
NEW STORY! FULL-COLOR GRAPHIC NOVEL
HARDY BOYS
#7
PAPERCUTZ

#7 "The Opposite Numbers"

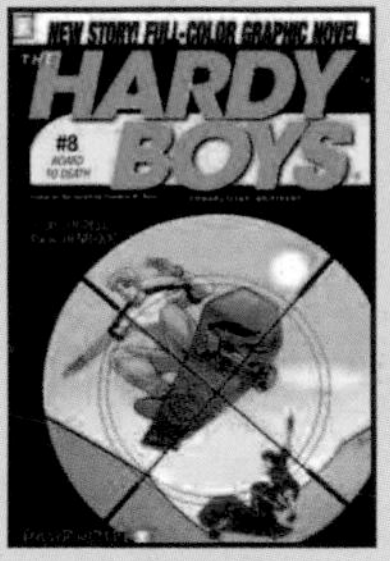
NEW STORY! FULL-COLOR GRAPHIC NOVEL
HARDY BOYS
#8

#8 "Board To Death"

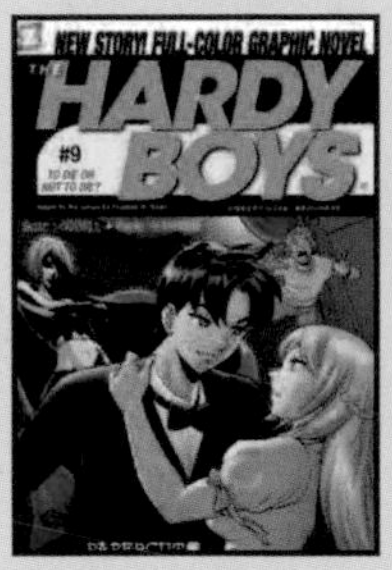
NEW STORY! FULL-COLOR GRAPHIC NOVEL
HARDY BOYS
#9

#9 "To Die Or Not To Die?"

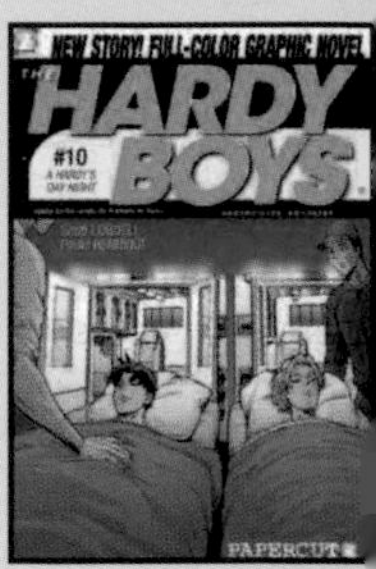
NEW STORY! FULL-COLOR GRAPHIC NOVEL
HARDY BOYS
#10
PAPERCUTZ

#10 "A Hardy Day's Night"

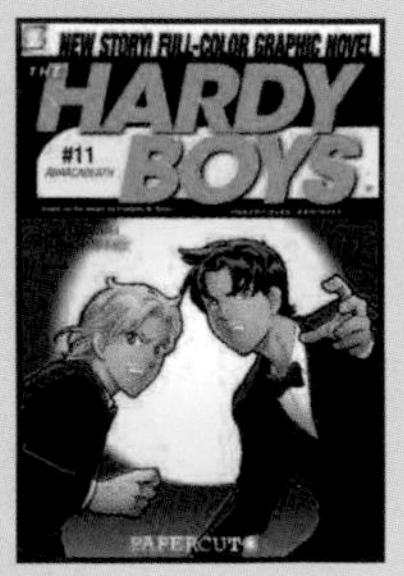
NEW STORY! FULL-COLOR GRAPHIC NOVEL
HARDY BOYS
#11
PAPERCUTZ

#11 "Abracadeath"

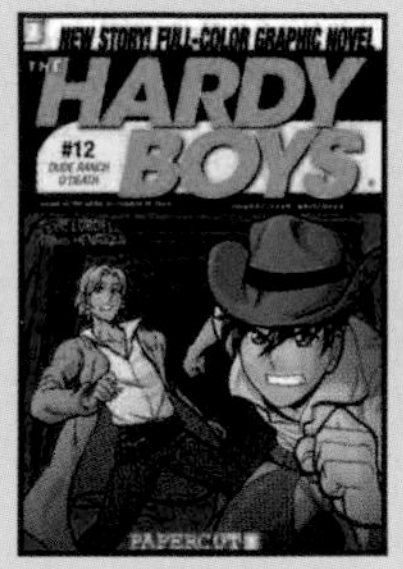
NEW STORY! FULL-COLOR GRAPHIC NOVEL
HARDY BOYS
#12
PAPERCUTZ

#12 "Dude Ranch O' Death!"

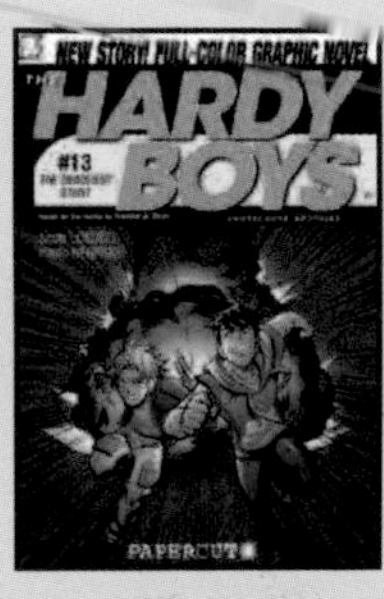
NEW STORY! FULL-COLOR GRAPHIC NOVEL
HARDY BOYS
#13
PAPERCUTZ

#13 "The Deadliest Stunt"

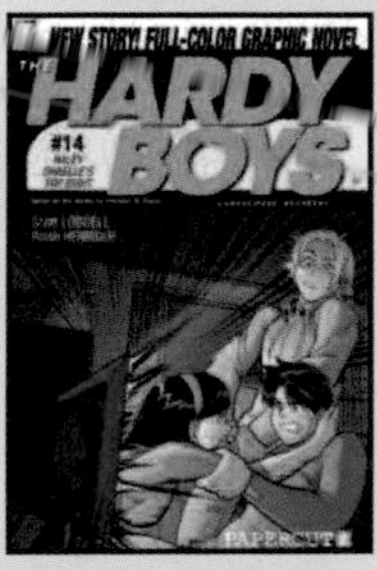
NEW STORY! FULL-COLOR GRAPHIC NOVEL
HARDY BOYS
#14
PAPERCUTZ

#14 "Haley Danielle's Top Eight!"

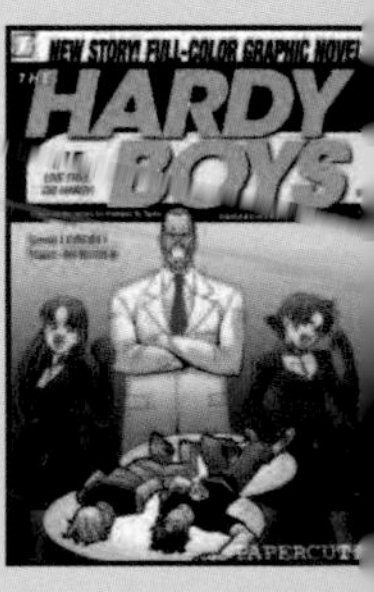
NEW STORY! FULL-COLOR GRAPHIC NOVEL
HARDY BOYS
PAPERCUTZ

#15 "Live Free, Die Hardy!"

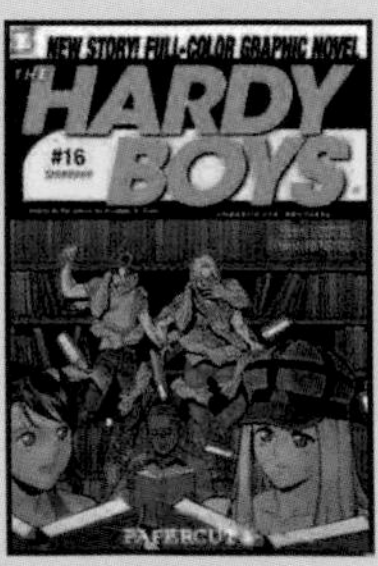
NEW STORY! FULL-COLOR GRAPHIC NOVEL
HARDY BOYS
#16
PAPERCUTZ

#16 "Shhhhhh!"

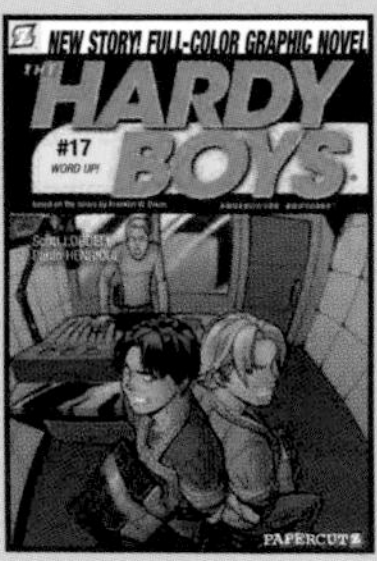
NEW STORY! FULL-COLOR GRAPHIC NOVEL
HARDY BOYS
#17
PAPERCUTZ

#17 "Word Up!"

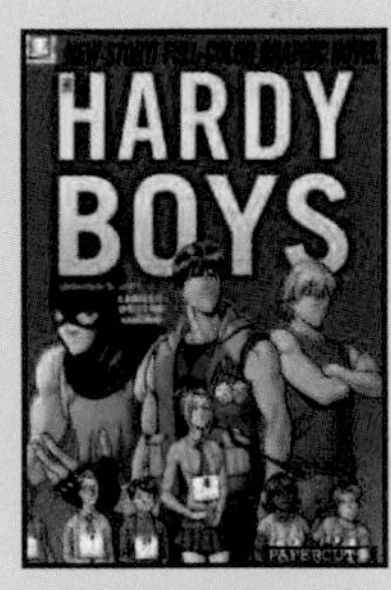
HARDY BOYS
PAPERCUTZ

#18 "D.A.N.G.E.R Spells the Hangman"

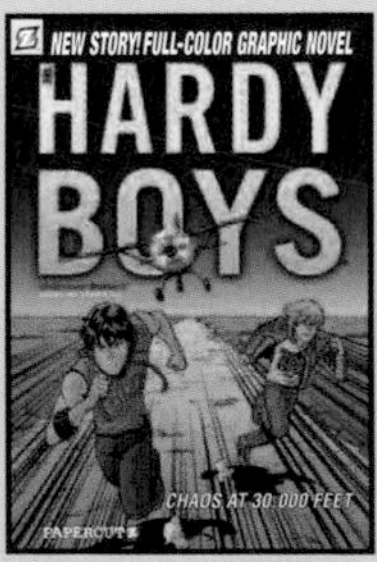
NEW STORY! FULL-COLOR GRAPHIC NOVEL
HARDY BOYS
CHAOS AT 30,000 FEET
PAPERCUTZ

#19 "Chaos at 30,000 Feet"

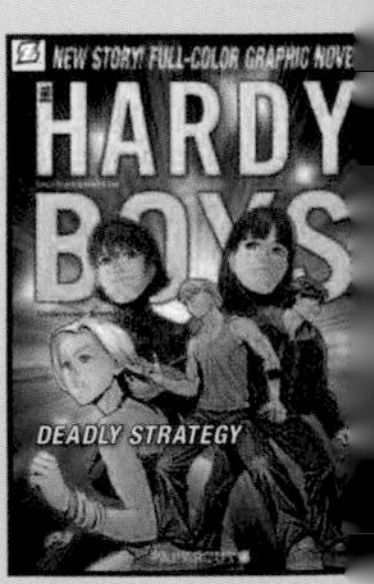
NEW STORY! FULL-COLOR GRAPHIC NOVEL
HARDY BOYS
DEADLY STRATEGY

#20 "Deadly Strategy"

$7.95 each in paperback, $12.95 each in hardcover except #20, $8.99 pb/$13.99 hc. Please add $4.00 for postage and handling for the first book, add $1.00 for each additional book. Please make check payable to NBM Publishing. Send to: **Papercutz, 40 Exchange Place, Suite 1308, New York, NY 10005 • 1-800-886-1223 • www.papercutz.com**

THE HARDY BOYS
THE NEW CASE FILES
Undercover Brothers

Crawling with
ZOMBIES

GERRY CONWAY
Writer

PAULO HENRIQUE
Artist

Based on the series by FRANKLIN W. DIXON

PAPERCUTZ™
New York

AMERICAN TEENAGERS AGAINST CRIME

A.T.A.C.

"Crawling With Zombies"
GERRY CONWAY - Writer
PAULO HENRIQUE - Artist
LAURIE E. SMITH - Colorist
MARK LERER - Letterer
JUNTO CREATIVE - Production

MICHAEL PETRANEK
Associate Editor
JIM SALICRUP
Editor-in-Chief

ISBN: 978-1-59707-219-9 paperback edition
ISBN: 978-1-59707-220-5 hardcover edition

Printed in China
August 2010 by Regent Publishing
6/f, Hang Tung Resource Centre
No. 18 A Kung Ngam Village Road
Shau Kei Wan, Hong Kong

Distributed by Macmillan.
First Printing

CHAPTER ONE: SPEED TRAP

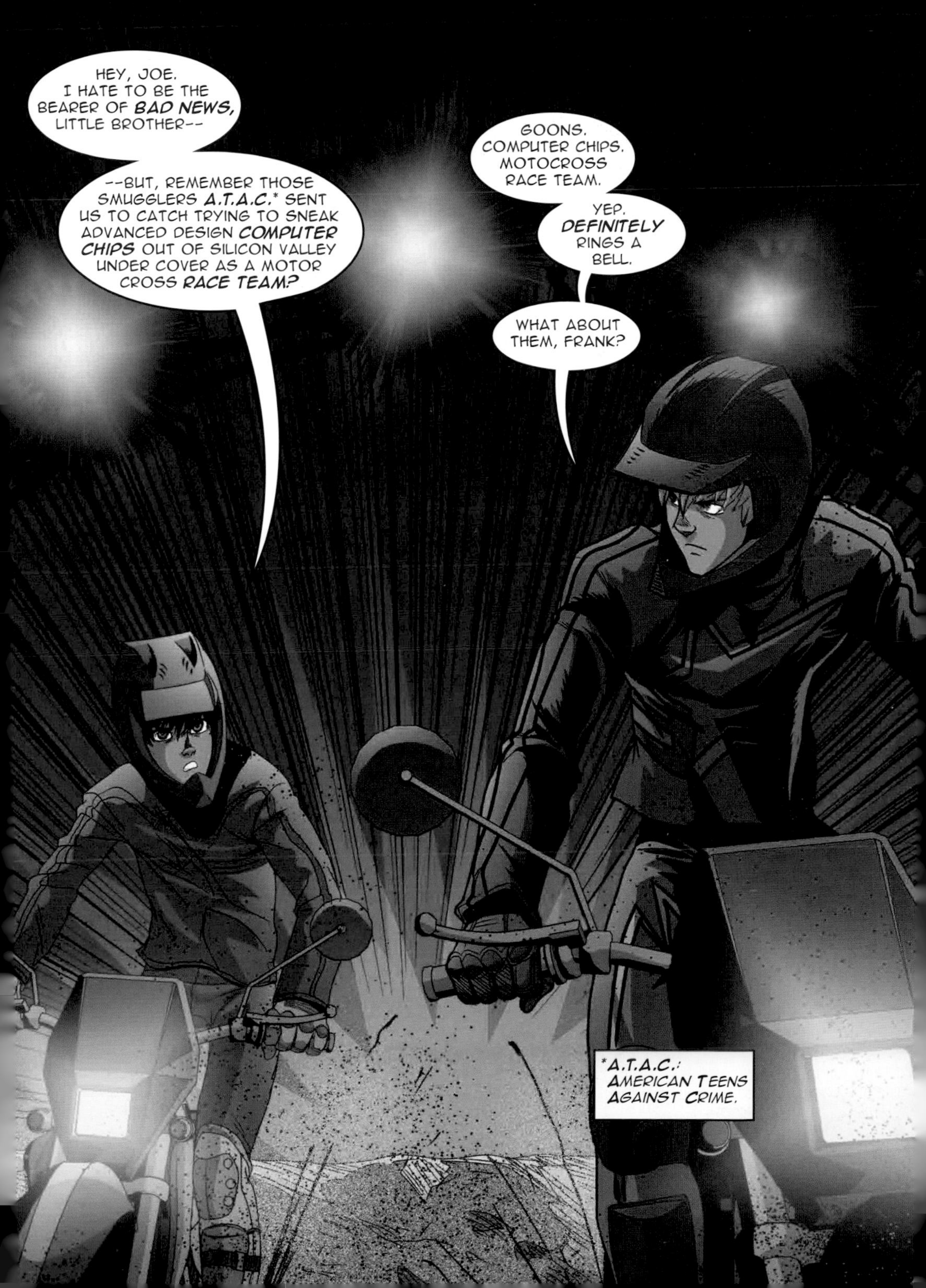
HEY, JOE. I HATE TO BE THE BEARER OF BAD NEWS, LITTLE BROTHER--
--BUT, REMEMBER THOSE SMUGGLERS A.T.A.C.* SENT US TO CATCH TRYING TO SNEAK ADVANCED DESIGN COMPUTER CHIPS OUT OF SILICON VALLEY UNDER COVER AS A MOTOR CROSS RACE TEAM?
GOONS. COMPUTER CHIPS. MOTOCROSS RACE TEAM.
YEP. DEFINITELY RINGS A BELL.
WHAT ABOUT THEM, FRANK?
*A.T.A.C.: AMERICAN TEENS AGAINST CRIME.

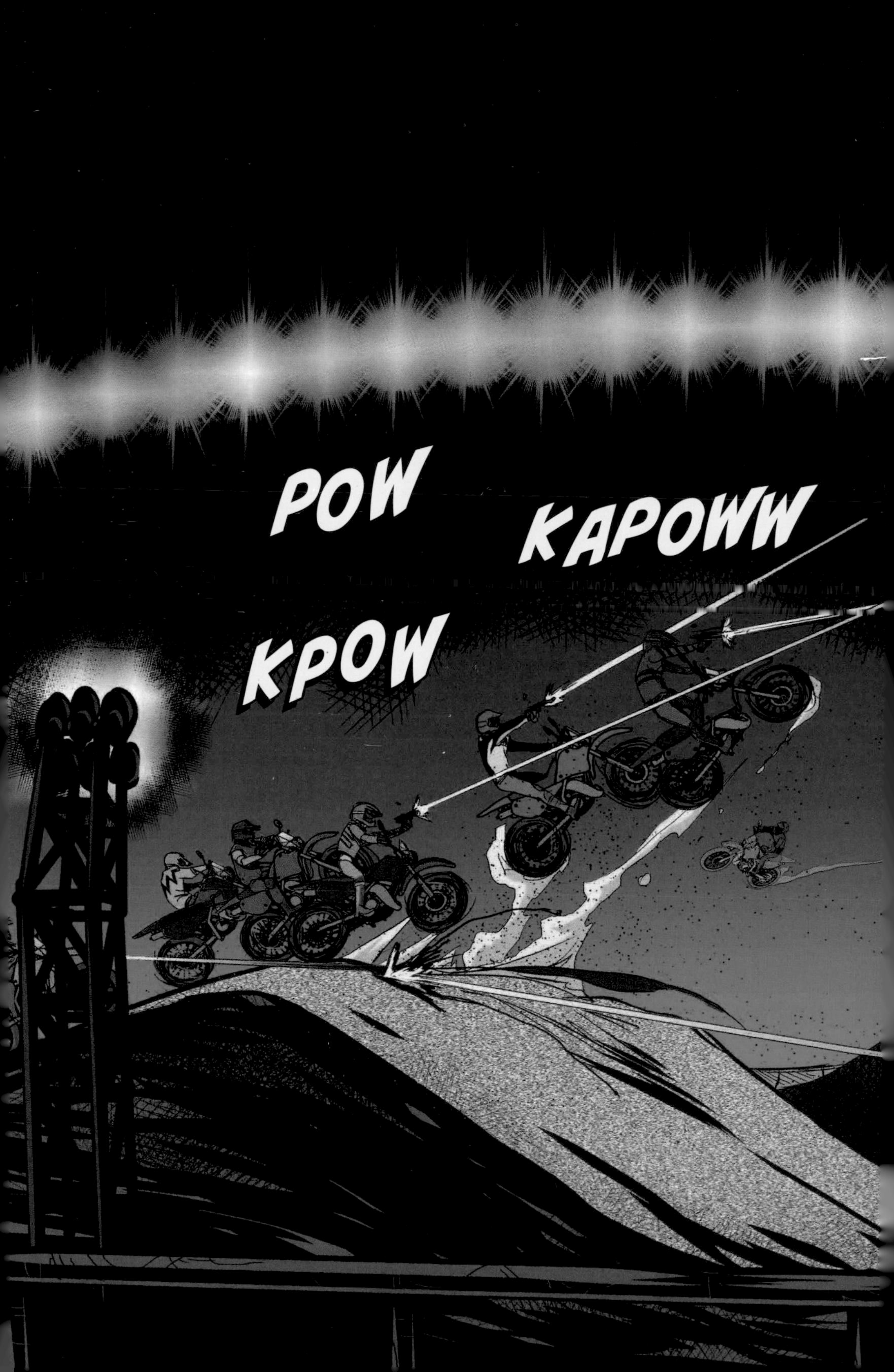
POW
KAPOWW
KPOW

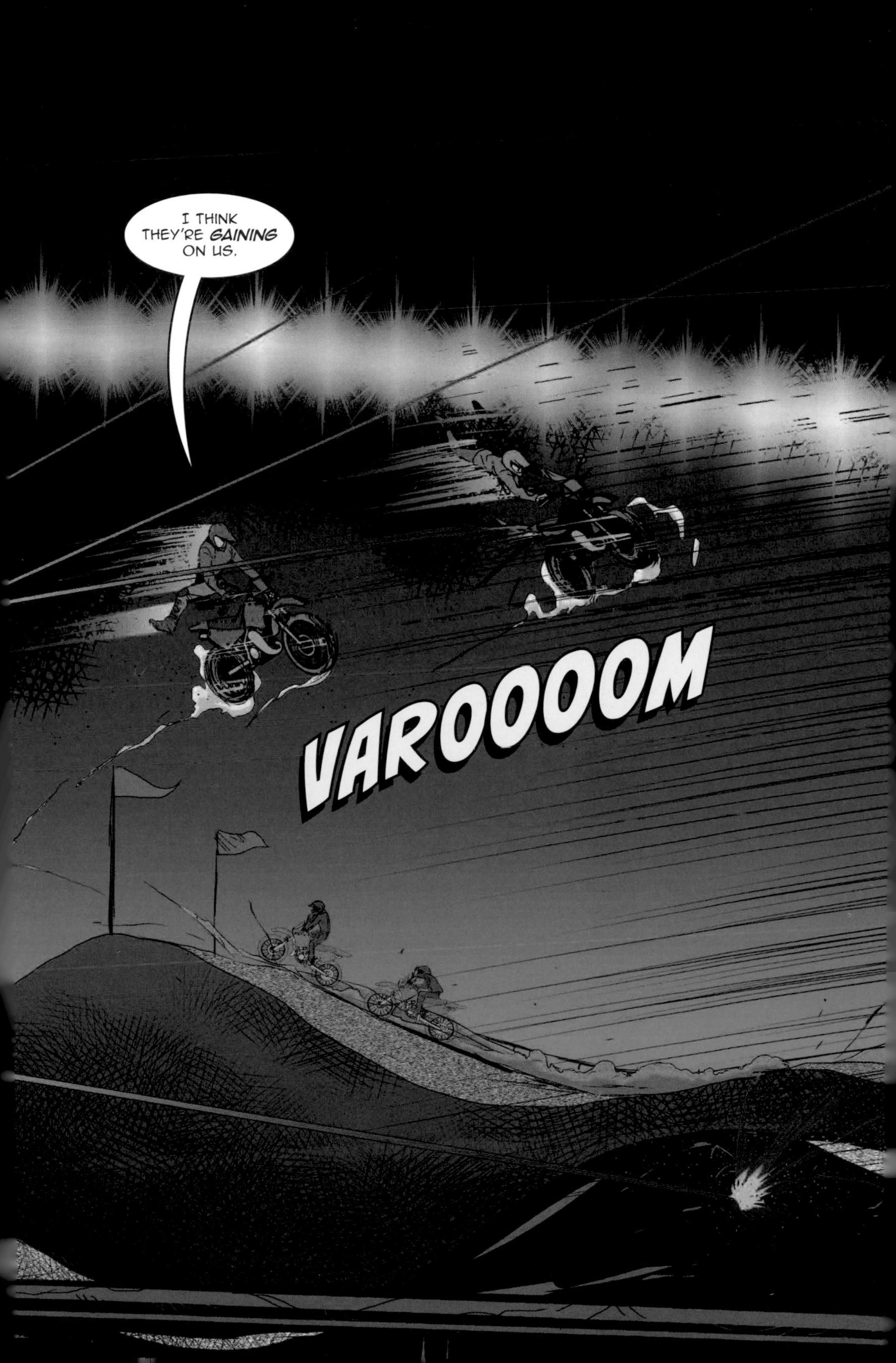
I THINK THEY'RE *GAINING* ON US.
VAROOOOM

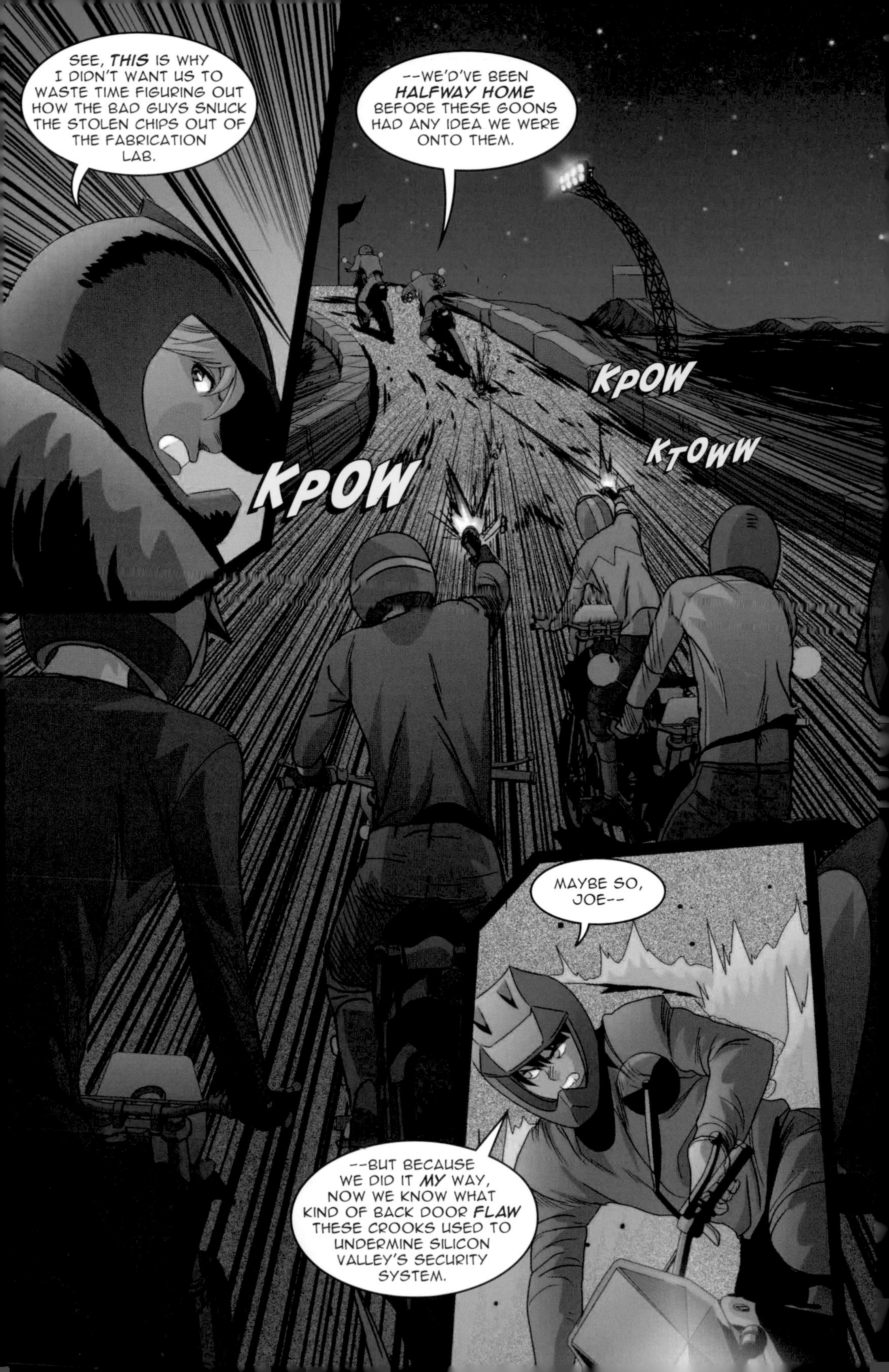
SEE, THIS IS WHY I DIDN'T WANT US TO WASTE TIME FIGURING OUT HOW THE BAD GUYS SNUCK THE STOLEN CHIPS OUT OF THE FABRICATION LAB.
--WE'D'VE BEEN HALFWAY HOME BEFORE THESE GOONS HAD ANY IDEA WE WERE ONTO THEM.
KPOW
KPOW
KTOWW
MAYBE SO, JOE--
--BUT BECAUSE WE DID IT MY WAY, NOW WE KNOW WHAT KIND OF BACK DOOR FLAW THESE CROOKS USED TO UNDERMINE SILICON VALLEY'S SECURITY SYSTEM.

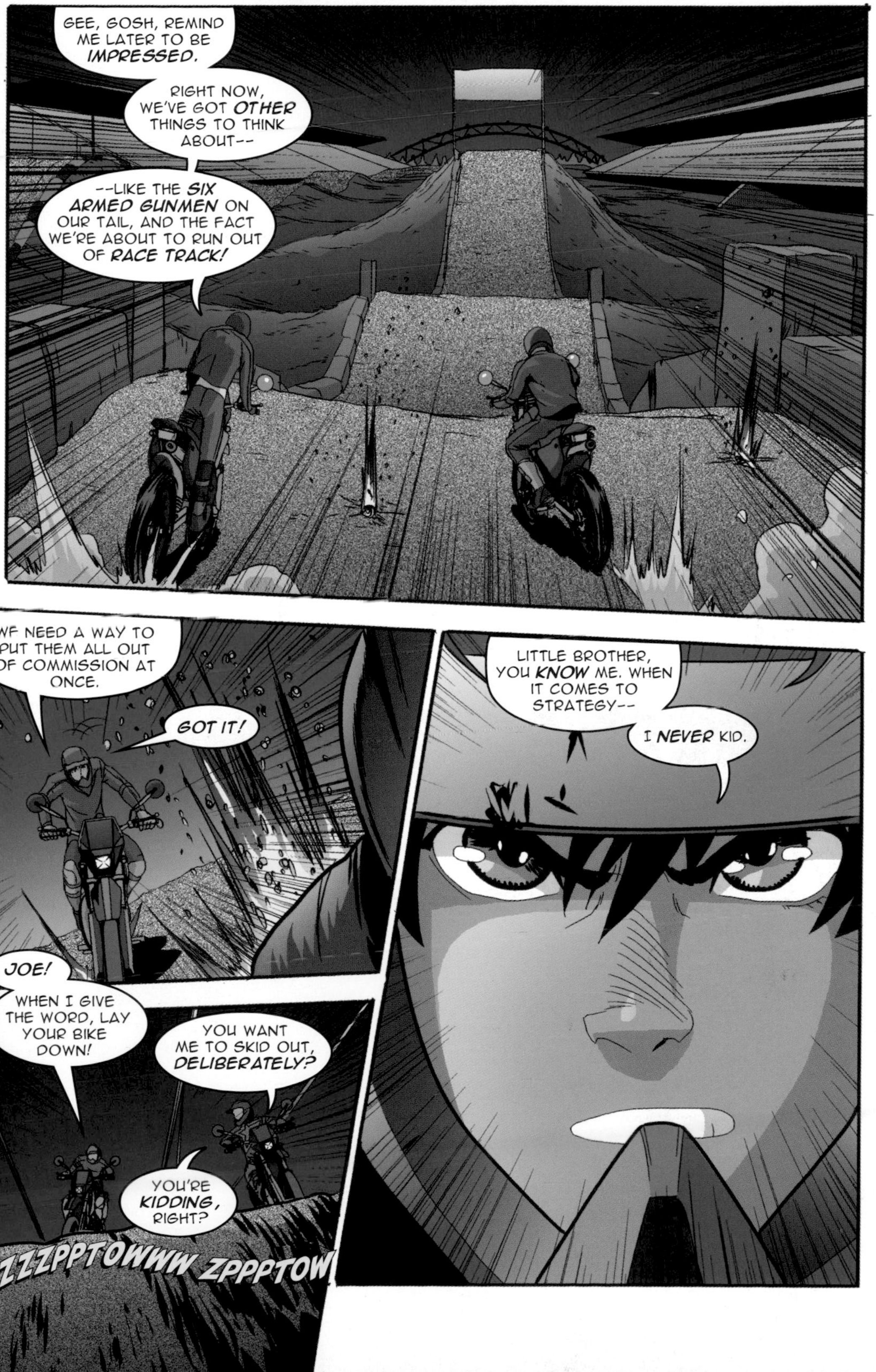
GEE, GOSH, REMIND ME LATER TO BE IMPRESSED.
RIGHT NOW, WE'VE GOT OTHER THINGS TO THINK ABOUT--
--LIKE THE SIX ARMED GUNMEN ON OUR TAIL, AND THE FACT WE'RE ABOUT TO RUN OUT OF RACE TRACK!
WE NEED A WAY TO PUT THEM ALL OUT OF COMMISSION AT ONCE.
GOT IT!
LITTLE BROTHER, YOU KNOW ME. WHEN IT COMES TO STRATEGY--
I NEVER KID.
JOE!
WHEN I GIVE THE WORD, LAY YOUR BIKE DOWN!
YOU WANT ME TO SKID OUT, DELIBERATELY?
YOU'RE KIDDING, RIGHT?
ZZZPPTOWWW ZPPPTOW

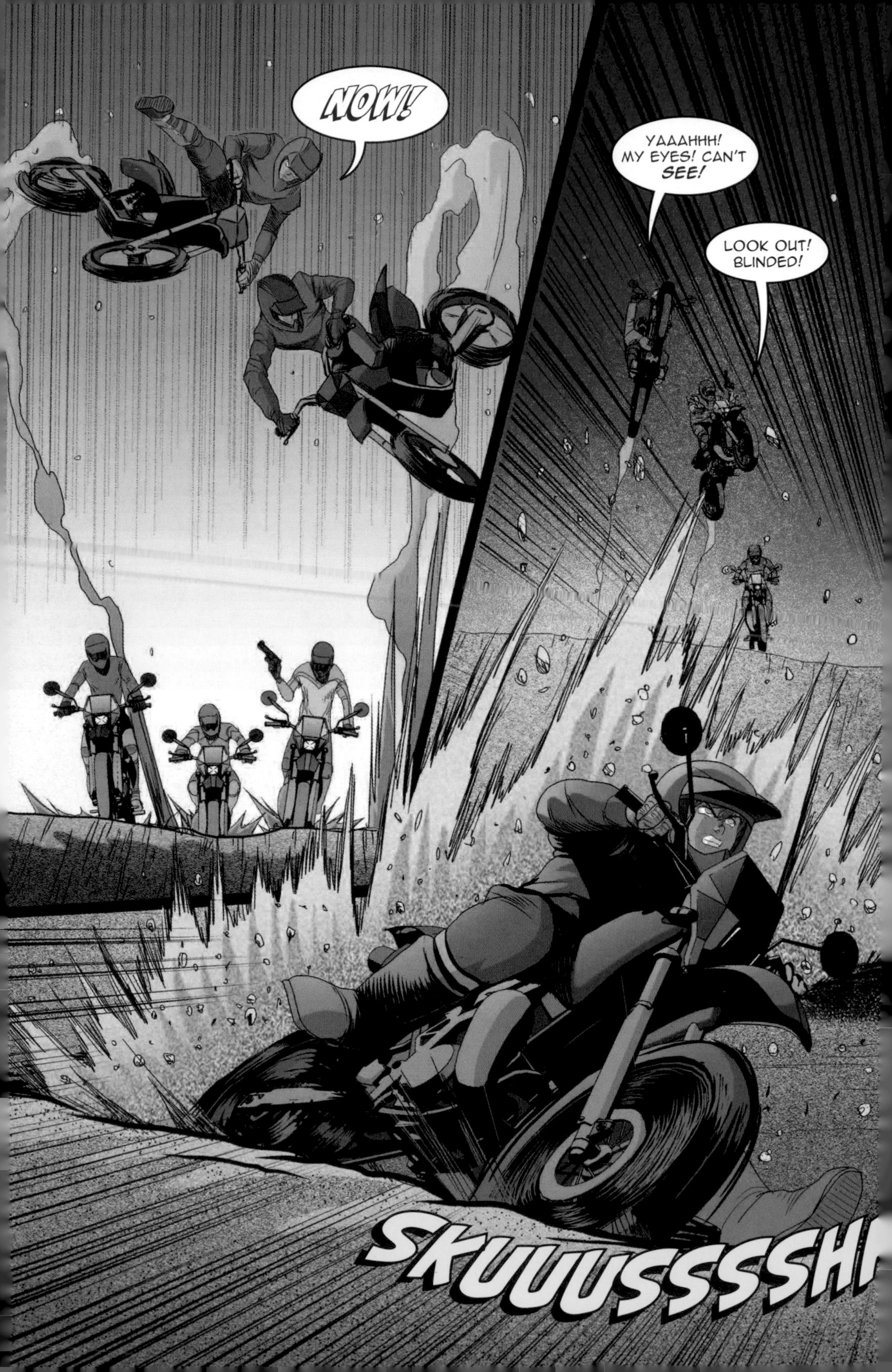
NOW!
YAAAHHH! MY EYES! CAN'T SEE!
LOOK OUT! BLINDED!
SKUUUSSSSH

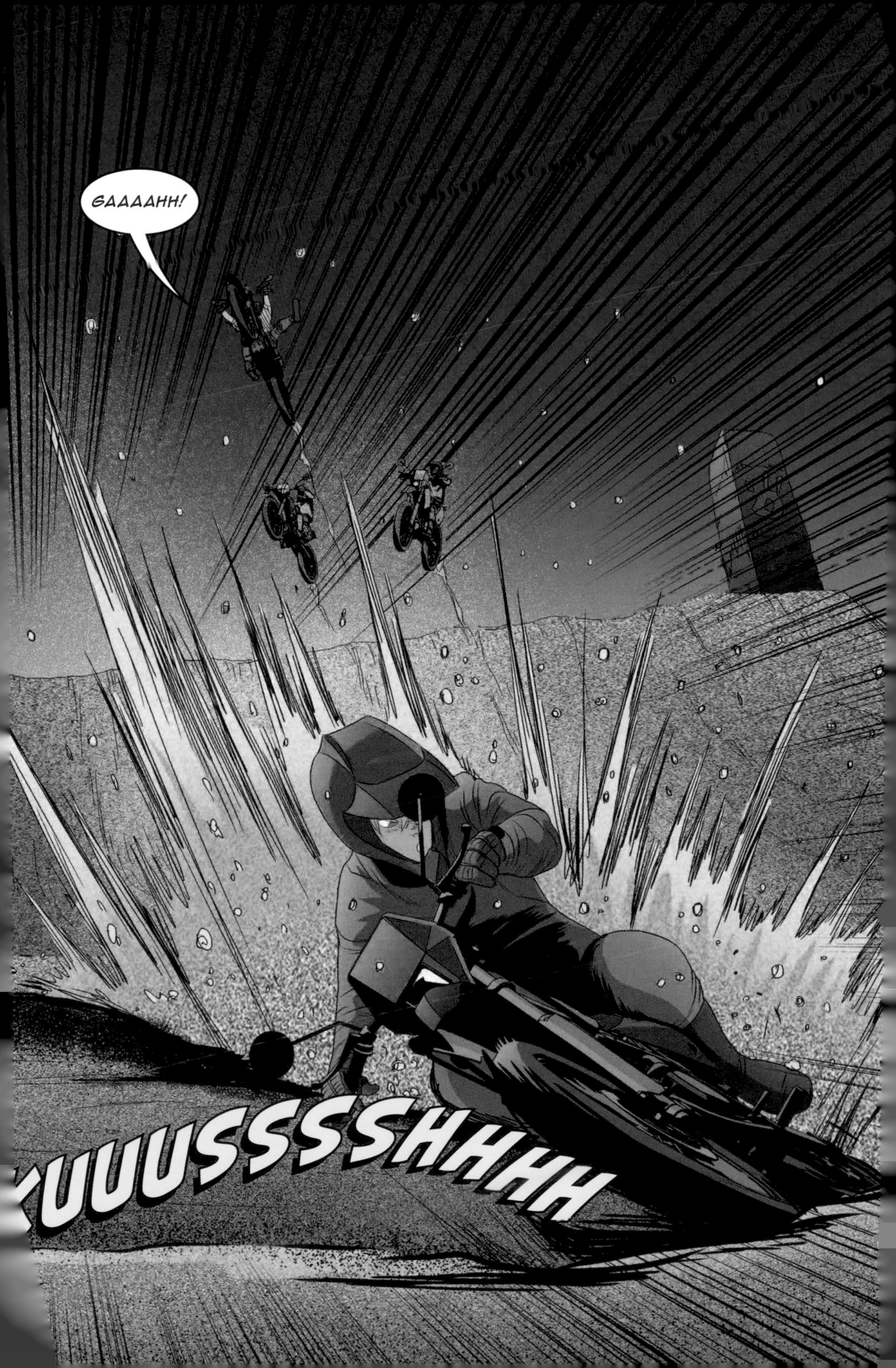
GAAAAHH!
ZUUUSSSSHHHH

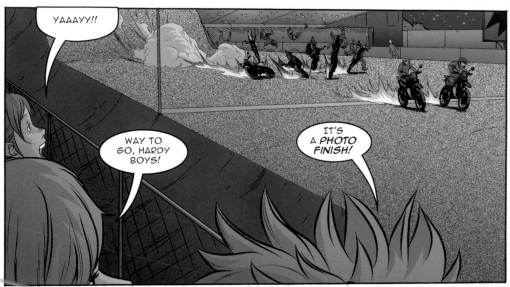

YAAAYY!!

WAY TO GO, HARDY BOYS!

IT'S A *PHOTO FINISH!*

GUESS WHAT, LITTLE BROTHER?

I THINK WE *WON.*

COULD YOU DO ME A FAVOR, FRANK?

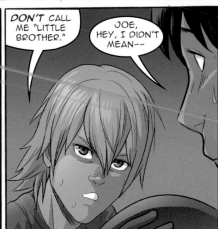

DON'T CALL ME "LITTLE BROTHER."

JOE, HEY, I DIDN'T MEAN--

YEAH, I KNOW YOU DIDN'T MEAN ANY- THING BY IT.

IT'S JUST, SOMETIMES...I GET *TIRED* OF BEING THE "YOUNGER HARDY BOY BROTHER."

WHAT'S GOING ON? WE GOT A REPORT OF *GUNSHOTS...*

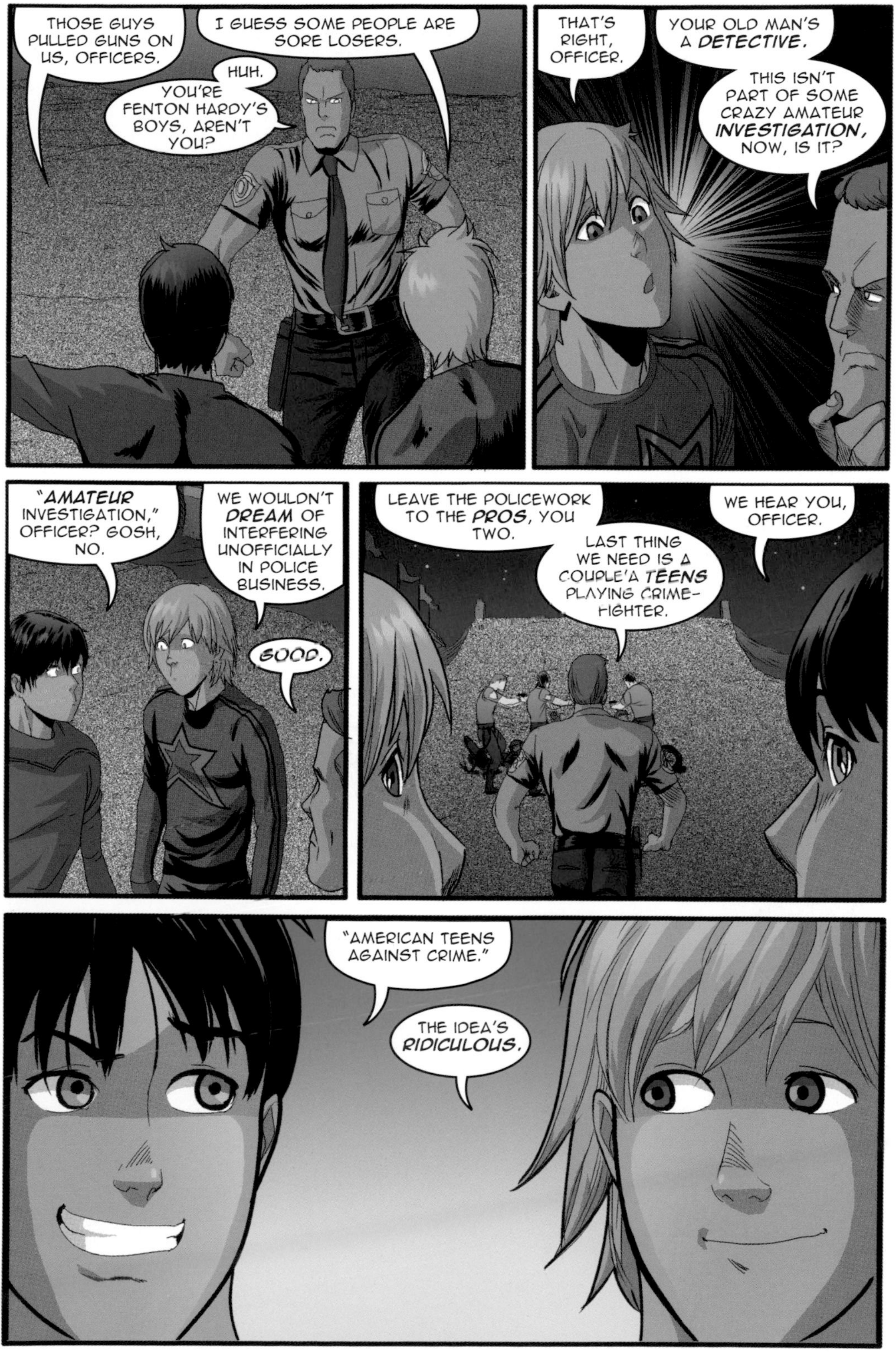
THOSE GUYS PULLED GUNS ON US, OFFICERS.
I GUESS SOME PEOPLE ARE SORE LOSERS.
HUH. YOU'RE FENTON HARDY'S BOYS, AREN'T YOU?
THAT'S RIGHT, OFFICER.
YOUR OLD MAN'S A DETECTIVE.
THIS ISN'T PART OF SOME CRAZY AMATEUR INVESTIGATION, NOW, IS IT?
"AMATEUR INVESTIGATION," OFFICER? GOSH, NO.
WE WOULDN'T DREAM OF INTERFERING UNOFFICIALLY IN POLICE BUSINESS.
GOOD.
LEAVE THE POLICEWORK TO THE PROS, YOU TWO.
LAST THING WE NEED IS A COUPLE'A TEENS PLAYING CRIME-FIGHTER.
WE HEAR YOU, OFFICER.
"AMERICAN TEENS AGAINST CRIME."
THE IDEA'S RIDICULOUS.

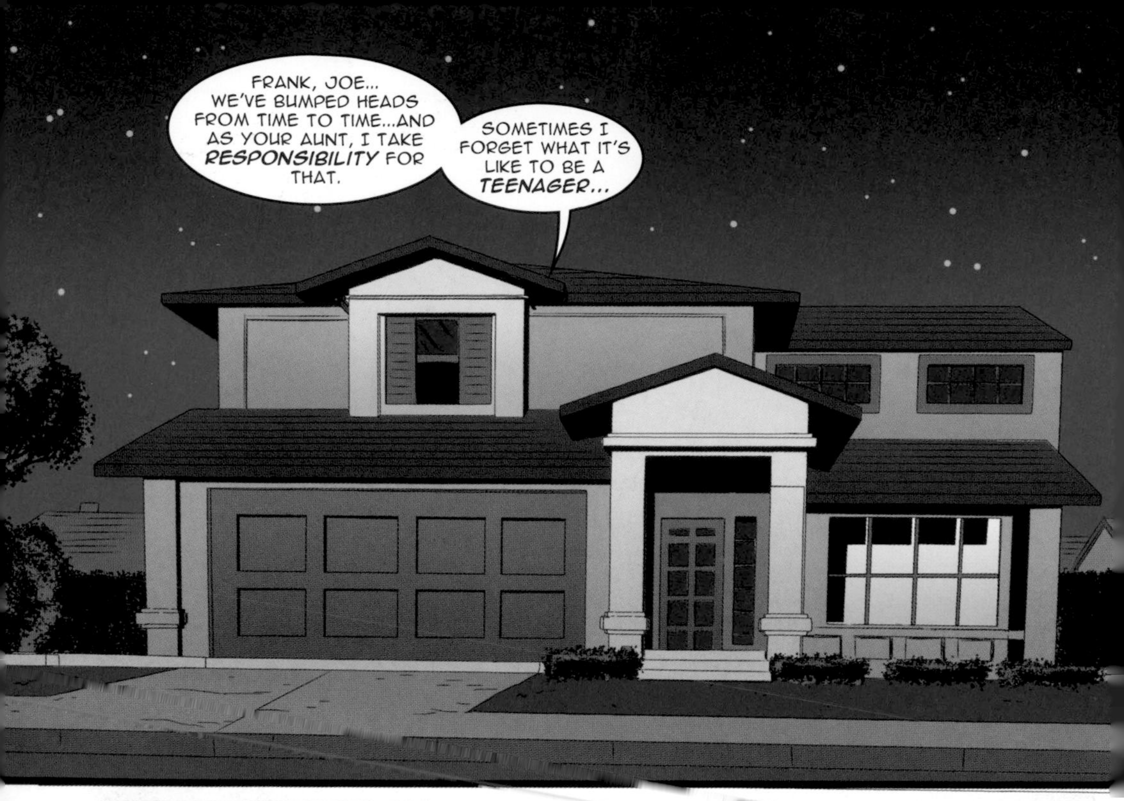
FRANK, JOE... WE'VE BUMPED HEADS FROM TIME TO TIME...AND AS YOUR AUNT, I TAKE *RESPONSIBILITY* FOR THAT.
SOMETIMES I FORGET WHAT IT'S LIKE TO BE A *TEENAGER...*

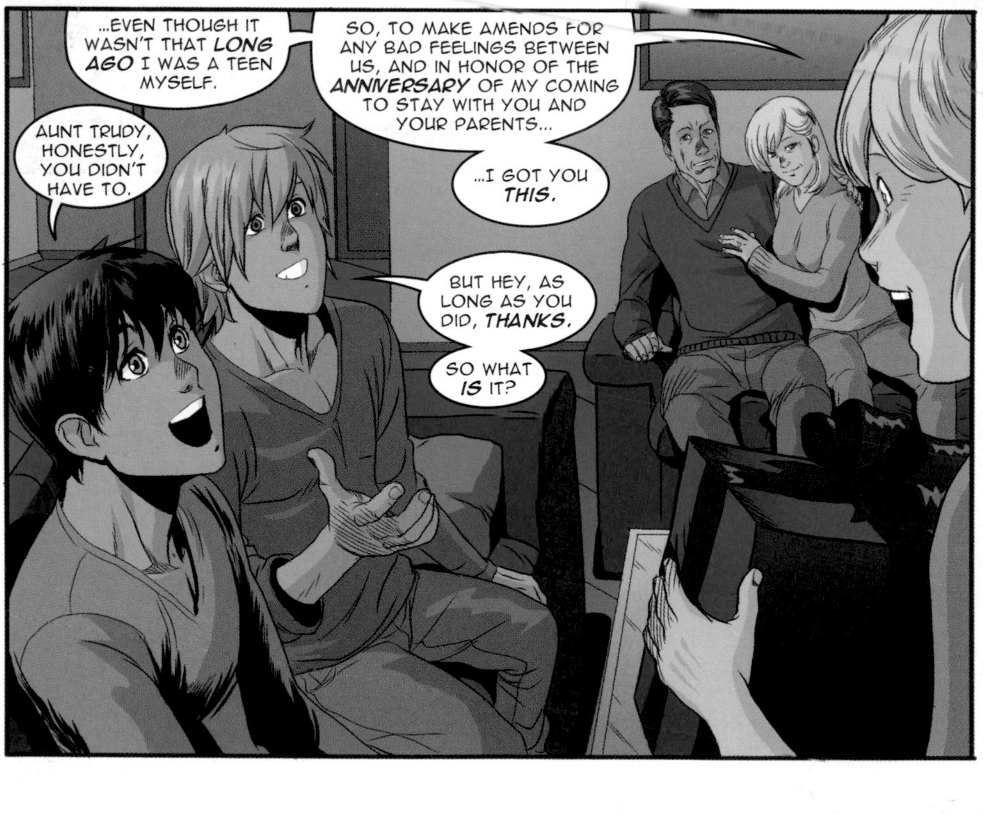
...EVEN THOUGH IT WASN'T THAT *LONG AGO* I WAS A TEEN MYSELF.
SO, TO MAKE AMENDS FOR ANY BAD FEELINGS BETWEEN US, AND IN HONOR OF THE *ANNIVERSARY* OF MY COMING TO STAY WITH YOU AND YOUR PARENTS...
...I GOT YOU *THIS.*
AUNT TRUDY, HONESTLY, YOU DIDN'T HAVE TO.
BUT HEY, AS LONG AS YOU DID, *THANKS.*
SO WHAT *IS* IT?

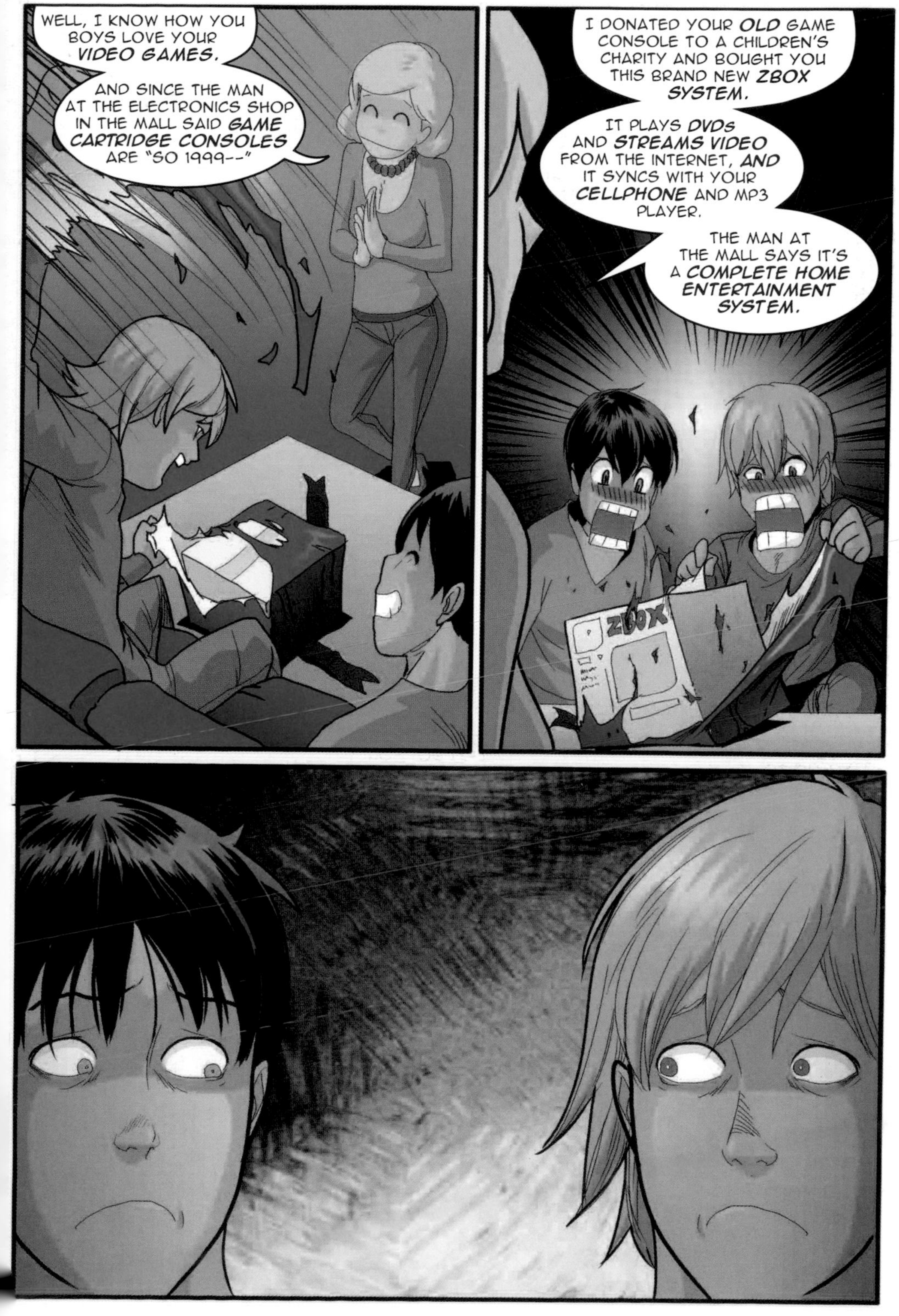
WELL, I KNOW HOW YOU BOYS LOVE YOUR VIDEO GAMES.
AND SINCE THE MAN AT THE ELECTRONICS SHOP IN THE MALL SAID GAME CARTRIDGE CONSOLES ARE "SO 1999--"
I DONATED YOUR OLD GAME CONSOLE TO A CHILDREN'S CHARITY AND BOUGHT YOU THIS BRAND NEW ZBOX SYSTEM.
IT PLAYS DVDs AND STREAMS VIDEO FROM THE INTERNET, AND IT SYNCS WITH YOUR CELLPHONE AND MP3 PLAYER.
THE MAN AT THE MALL SAYS IT'S A COMPLETE HOME ENTERTAINMENT SYSTEM.
ZBOX

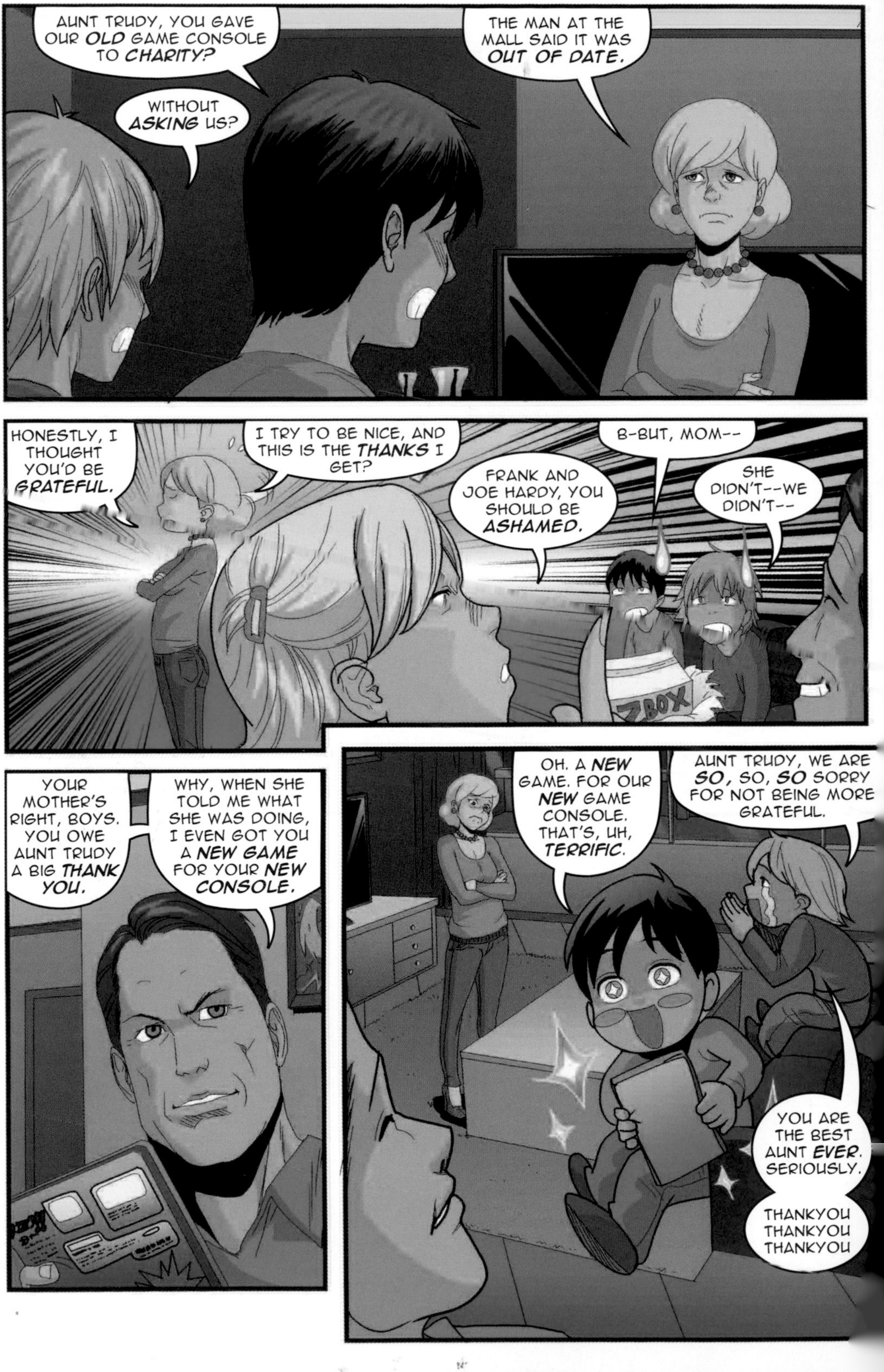

AUNT TRUDY, YOU GAVE OUR **OLD** GAME CONSOLE TO **CHARITY?**
WITHOUT **ASKING** US?
THE MAN AT THE MALL SAID IT WAS **OUT OF DATE.**
HONESTLY, I THOUGHT YOU'D BE **GRATEFUL.**
I TRY TO BE NICE, AND THIS IS THE **THANKS** I GET?
FRANK AND JOE HARDY, YOU SHOULD BE **ASHAMED.**
B-BUT, MOM--
SHE DIDN'T--WE DIDN'T--
ZBOX
YOUR MOTHER'S RIGHT, BOYS. YOU OWE AUNT TRUDY A BIG **THANK YOU.**
WHY, WHEN SHE TOLD ME WHAT SHE WAS DOING, I EVEN GOT YOU A **NEW GAME** FOR YOUR **NEW CONSOLE.**
OH. A **NEW** GAME. FOR OUR **NEW** GAME CONSOLE. THAT'S, UH, **TERRIFIC.**
AUNT TRUDY, WE ARE **SO,** SO, **SO** SORRY FOR NOT BEING MORE GRATEFUL.
YOU ARE THE BEST AUNT **EVER.** SERIOUSLY.
THANKYOU THANKYOU THANKYOU

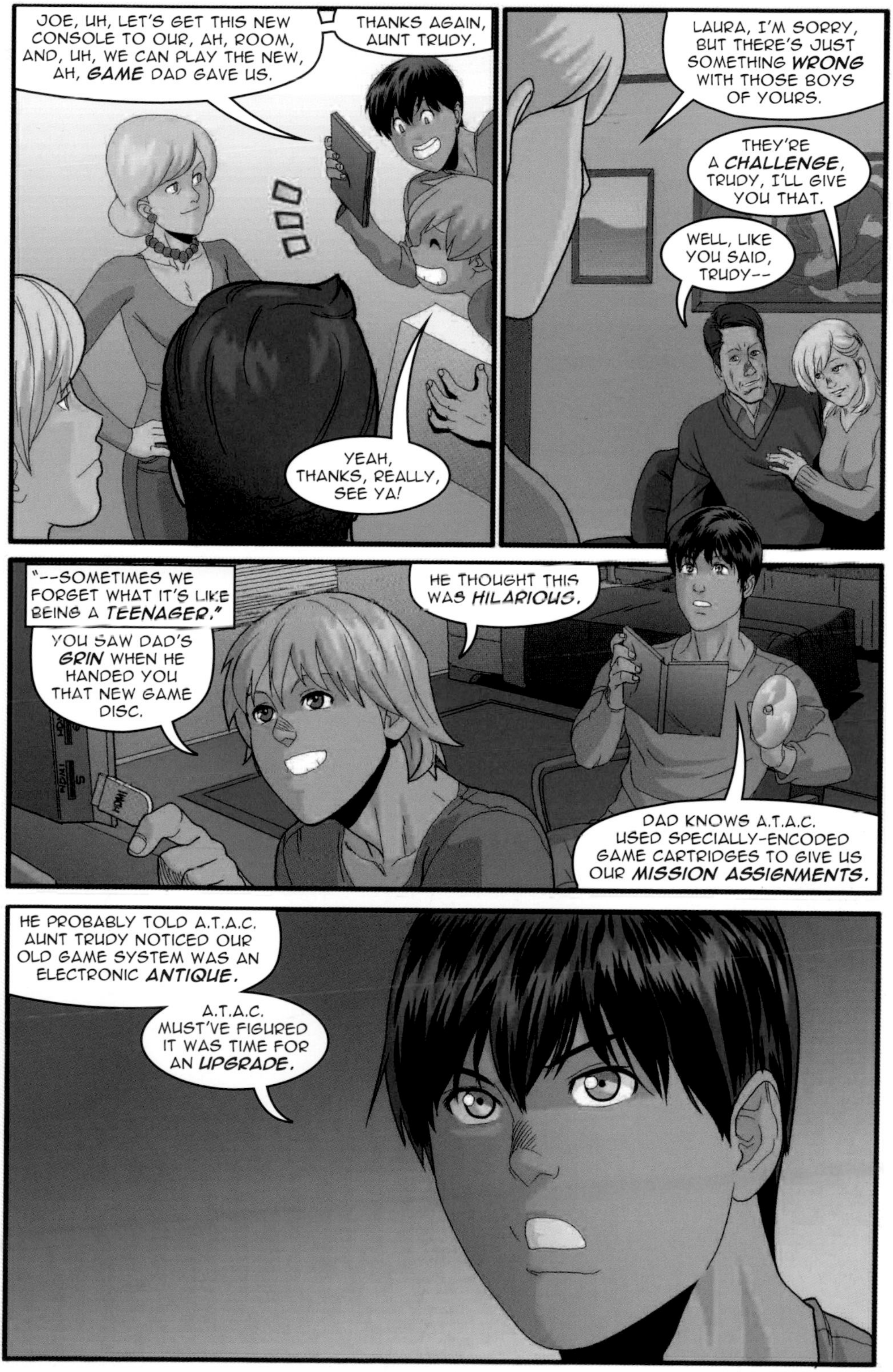
JOE, UH, LET'S GET THIS NEW CONSOLE TO OUR, AH, ROOM, AND, UH, WE CAN PLAY THE NEW, AH, GAME DAD GAVE US.
THANKS AGAIN, AUNT TRUDY.
YEAH, THANKS, REALLY, SEE YA!
LAURA, I'M SORRY, BUT THERE'S JUST SOMETHING WRONG WITH THOSE BOYS OF YOURS.
THEY'RE A CHALLENGE, TRUDY, I'LL GIVE YOU THAT.
WELL, LIKE YOU SAID, TRUDY--
"--SOMETIMES WE FORGET WHAT IT'S LIKE BEING A TEENAGER."
YOU SAW DAD'S GRIN WHEN HE HANDED YOU THAT NEW GAME DISC.
HE THOUGHT THIS WAS HILARIOUS.
DAD KNOWS A.T.A.C. USED SPECIALLY-ENCODED GAME CARTRIDGES TO GIVE US OUR MISSION ASSIGNMENTS.
HE PROBABLY TOLD A.T.A.C. AUNT TRUDY NOTICED OUR OLD GAME SYSTEM WAS AN ELECTRONIC ANTIQUE.
A.T.A.C. MUST'VE FIGURED IT WAS TIME FOR AN UPGRADE.

GREETINGS, HARDY BOYS.

AS YOU MAY KNOW, THANKS TO THE GROWTH OF ONLINE SOCIAL NETWORKING, IT'S EASIER THAN EVER FOR TEENS TO GATHER WITH FRIENDS AND OTHERS IN LARGE GROUPS CALLED **"FLASH MOBS."**

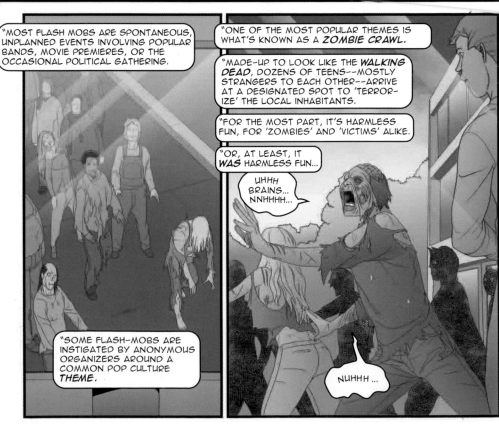

"MOST FLASH MOBS ARE SPONTANEOUS, UNPLANNED EVENTS INVOLVING POPULAR BANDS, MOVIE PREMIERES, OR THE OCCASIONAL POLITICAL GATHERING.

"SOME FLASH-MOBS ARE INSTIGATED BY ANONYMOUS ORGANIZERS AROUND A COMMON POP CULTURE **THEME**.

"ONE OF THE MOST POPULAR THEMES IS WHAT'S KNOWN AS A **ZOMBIE CRAWL.**

"MADE-UP TO LOOK LIKE THE **WALKING DEAD**, DOZENS OF TEENS--MOSTLY STRANGERS TO EACH OTHER--ARRIVE AT A DESIGNATED SPOT TO 'TERRORIZE' THE LOCAL INHABITANTS.

"FOR THE MOST PART, IT'S HARMLESS FUN, FOR 'ZOMBIES' AND 'VICTIMS' ALIKE.

"OR, AT LEAST, IT **WAS** HARMLESS FUN...

UHHH BRAINS... NNHHHH...

NUHHH ...

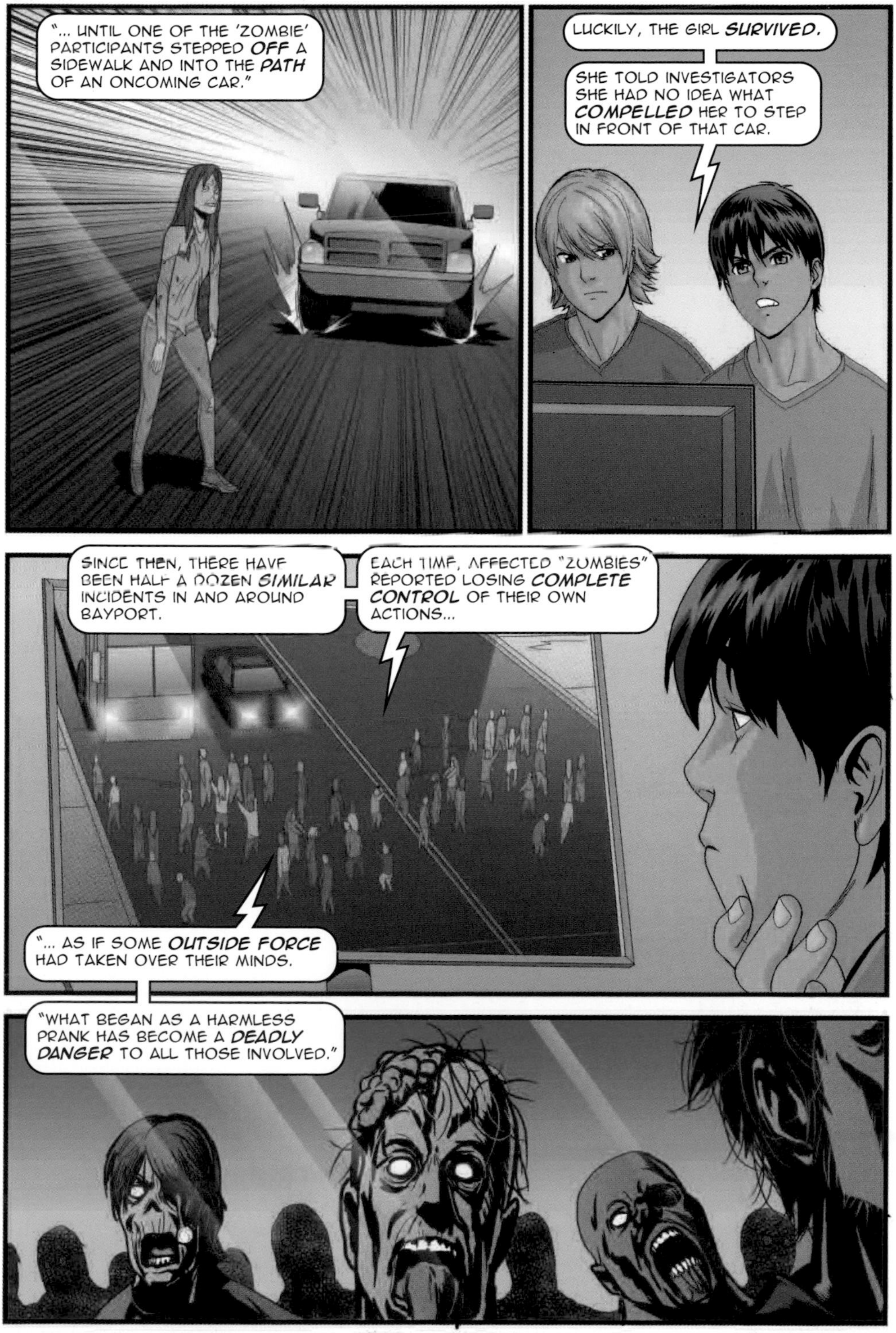
"... UNTIL ONE OF THE 'ZOMBIE' PARTICIPANTS STEPPED OFF A SIDEWALK AND INTO THE PATH OF AN ONCOMING CAR."
LUCKILY, THE GIRL SURVIVED.
SHE TOLD INVESTIGATORS SHE HAD NO IDEA WHAT COMPELLED HER TO STEP IN FRONT OF THAT CAR.
SINCE THEN, THERE HAVE BEEN HALF A DOZEN SIMILAR INCIDENTS IN AND AROUND BAYPORT.
EACH TIME, AFFECTED "ZOMBIES" REPORTED LOSING COMPLETE CONTROL OF THEIR OWN ACTIONS...
"... AS IF SOME OUTSIDE FORCE HAD TAKEN OVER THEIR MINDS.
"WHAT BEGAN AS A HARMLESS PRANK HAS BECOME A DEADLY DANGER TO ALL THOSE INVOLVED."

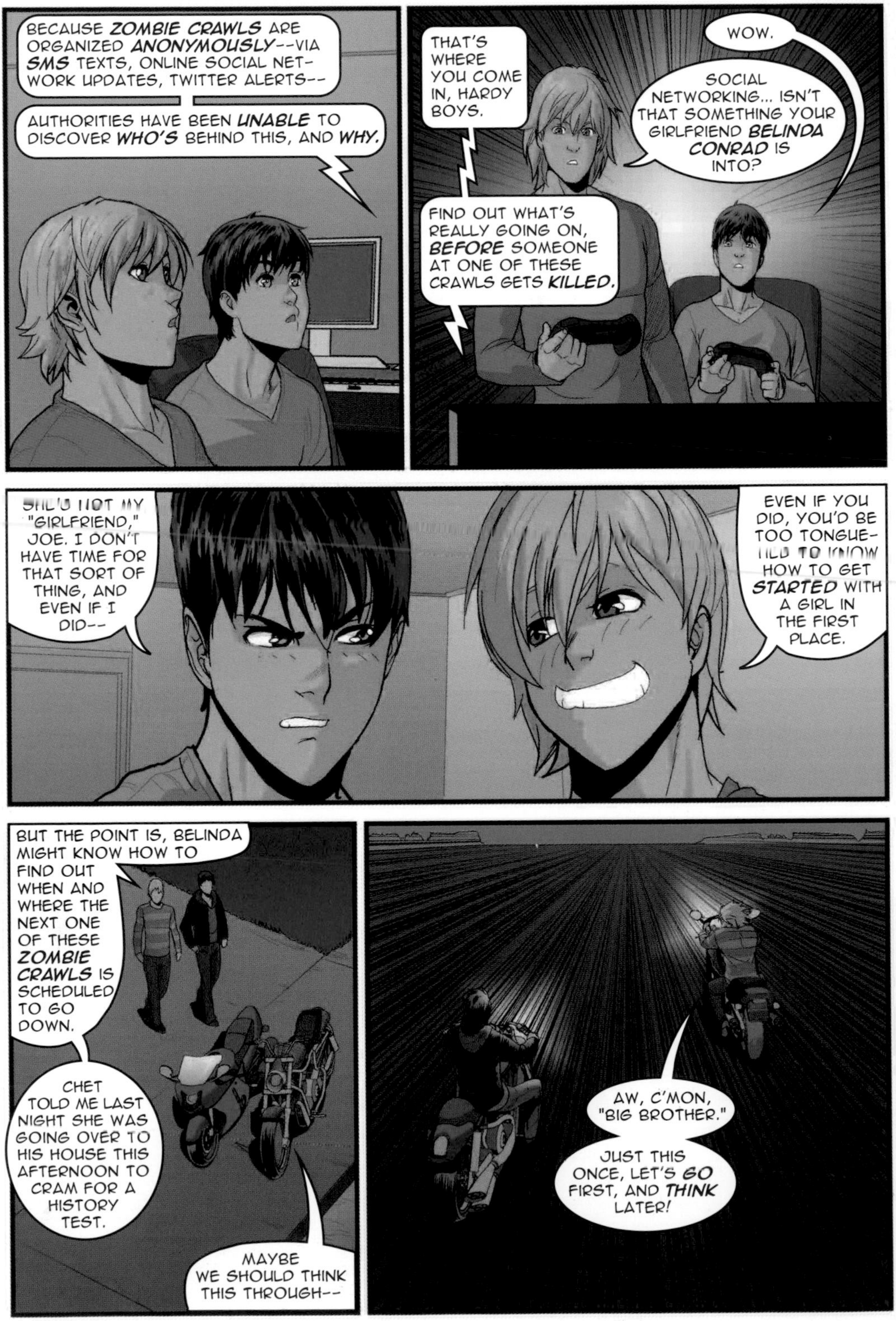
BECAUSE ZOMBIE CRAWLS ARE ORGANIZED ANONYMOUSLY--VIA SMS TEXTS, ONLINE SOCIAL NETWORK UPDATES, TWITTER ALERTS--
AUTHORITIES HAVE BEEN UNABLE TO DISCOVER WHO'S BEHIND THIS, AND WHY.
THAT'S WHERE YOU COME IN, HARDY BOYS.
FIND OUT WHAT'S REALLY GOING ON, BEFORE SOMEONE AT ONE OF THESE CRAWLS GETS KILLED.
WOW.
SOCIAL NETWORKING... ISN'T THAT SOMETHING YOUR GIRLFRIEND BELINDA CONRAD IS INTO?
SHE'S NOT MY "GIRLFRIEND," JOE. I DON'T HAVE TIME FOR THAT SORT OF THING, AND EVEN IF I DID--
EVEN IF YOU DID, YOU'D BE TOO TONGUE-TIED TO KNOW HOW TO GET STARTED WITH A GIRL IN THE FIRST PLACE.
BUT THE POINT IS, BELINDA MIGHT KNOW HOW TO FIND OUT WHEN AND WHERE THE NEXT ONE OF THESE ZOMBIE CRAWLS IS SCHEDULED TO GO DOWN.
CHET TOLD ME LAST NIGHT SHE WAS GOING OVER TO HIS HOUSE THIS AFTERNOON TO CRAM FOR A HISTORY TEST.
MAYBE WE SHOULD THINK THIS THROUGH--
AW, C'MON, "BIG BROTHER."
JUST THIS ONCE, LET'S GO FIRST, AND THINK LATER!

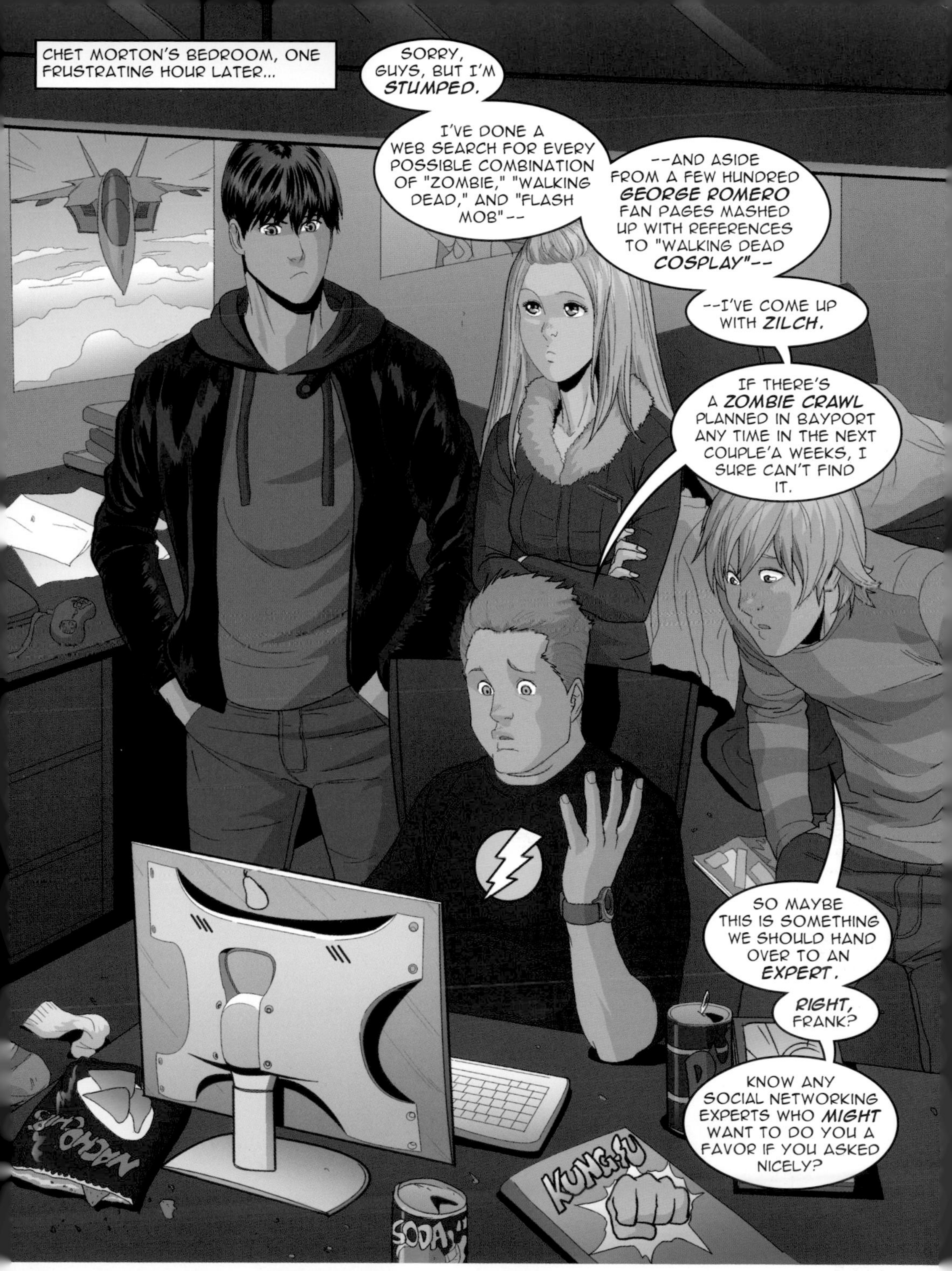

CHET MORTON'S BEDROOM, ONE FRUSTRATING HOUR LATER...
SORRY, GUYS, BUT I'M STUMPED.
I'VE DONE A WEB SEARCH FOR EVERY POSSIBLE COMBINATION OF "ZOMBIE," "WALKING DEAD," AND "FLASH MOB"--
--AND ASIDE FROM A FEW HUNDRED GEORGE ROMERO FAN PAGES MASHED UP WITH REFERENCES TO "WALKING DEAD COSPLAY"--
--I'VE COME UP WITH ZILCH.
IF THERE'S A ZOMBIE CRAWL PLANNED IN BAYPORT ANY TIME IN THE NEXT COUPLE'A WEEKS, I SURE CAN'T FIND IT.
SO MAYBE THIS IS SOMETHING WE SHOULD HAND OVER TO AN EXPERT.
RIGHT, FRANK?
KNOW ANY SOCIAL NETWORKING EXPERTS WHO MIGHT WANT TO DO YOU A FAVOR IF YOU ASKED NICELY?
NACHO CHIPS
KUNG-FU
SODA

CHAPTER THREE: TWO'S COMPANY, THREE'S A CROWD

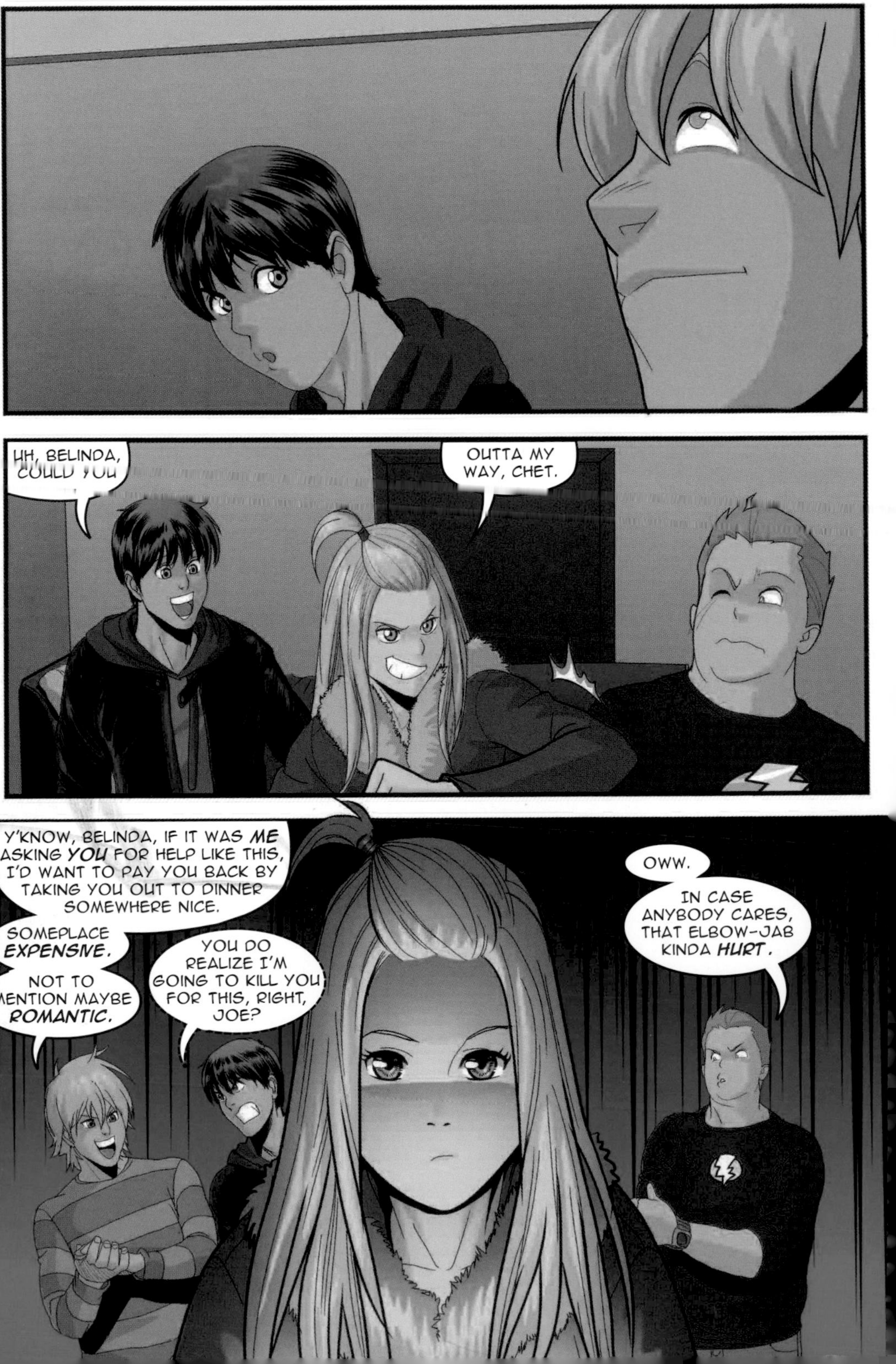
UH, BELINDA, COULD YOU
OUTTA MY WAY, CHET.
Y'KNOW, BELINDA, IF IT WAS **ME** ASKING **YOU** FOR HELP LIKE THIS, I'D WANT TO PAY YOU BACK BY TAKING YOU OUT TO DINNER SOMEWHERE NICE.
SOMEPLACE **EXPENSIVE**.
NOT TO MENTION MAYBE **ROMANTIC**.
YOU DO REALIZE I'M GOING TO KILL YOU FOR THIS, RIGHT, JOE?
OWW.
IN CASE ANYBODY CARES, THAT ELBOW-JAB KINDA **HURT**.

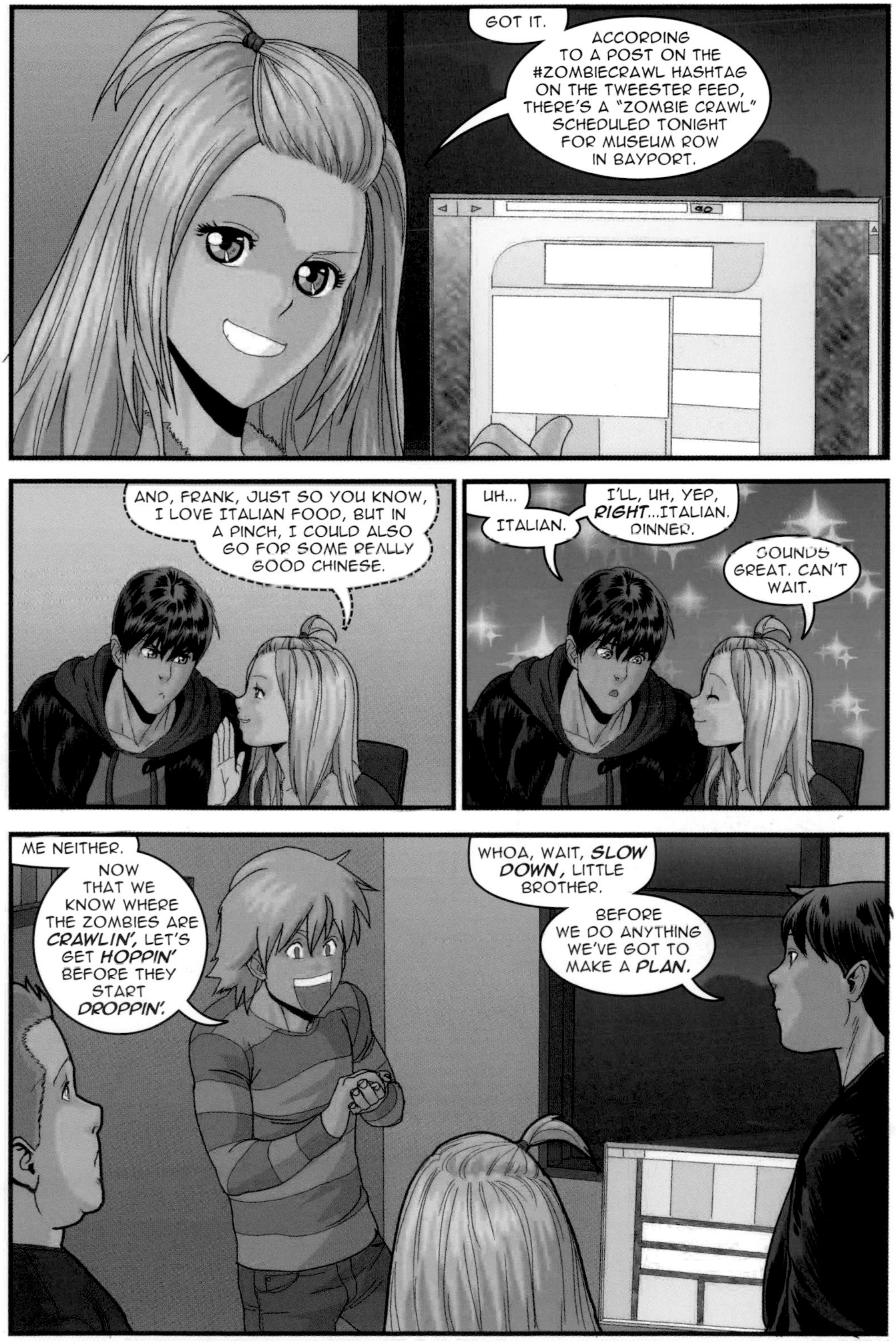

GOT IT.
ACCORDING TO A POST ON THE #ZOMBIECRAWL HASHTAG ON THE TWEESTER FEED, THERE'S A "ZOMBIE CRAWL" SCHEDULED TONIGHT FOR MUSEUM ROW IN BAYPORT.
GO
AND, FRANK, JUST SO YOU KNOW, I LOVE ITALIAN FOOD, BUT IN A PINCH, I COULD ALSO GO FOR SOME REALLY GOOD CHINESE.
UH...
ITALIAN.
I'LL, UH, YEP, RIGHT...ITALIAN. DINNER.
SOUNDS GREAT. CAN'T WAIT.
ME NEITHER.
NOW THAT WE KNOW WHERE THE ZOMBIES ARE CRAWLIN', LET'S GET HOPPIN' BEFORE THEY START DROPPIN'.
WHOA, WAIT, SLOW DOWN, LITTLE BROTHER.
BEFORE WE DO ANYTHING WE'VE GOT TO MAKE A PLAN.

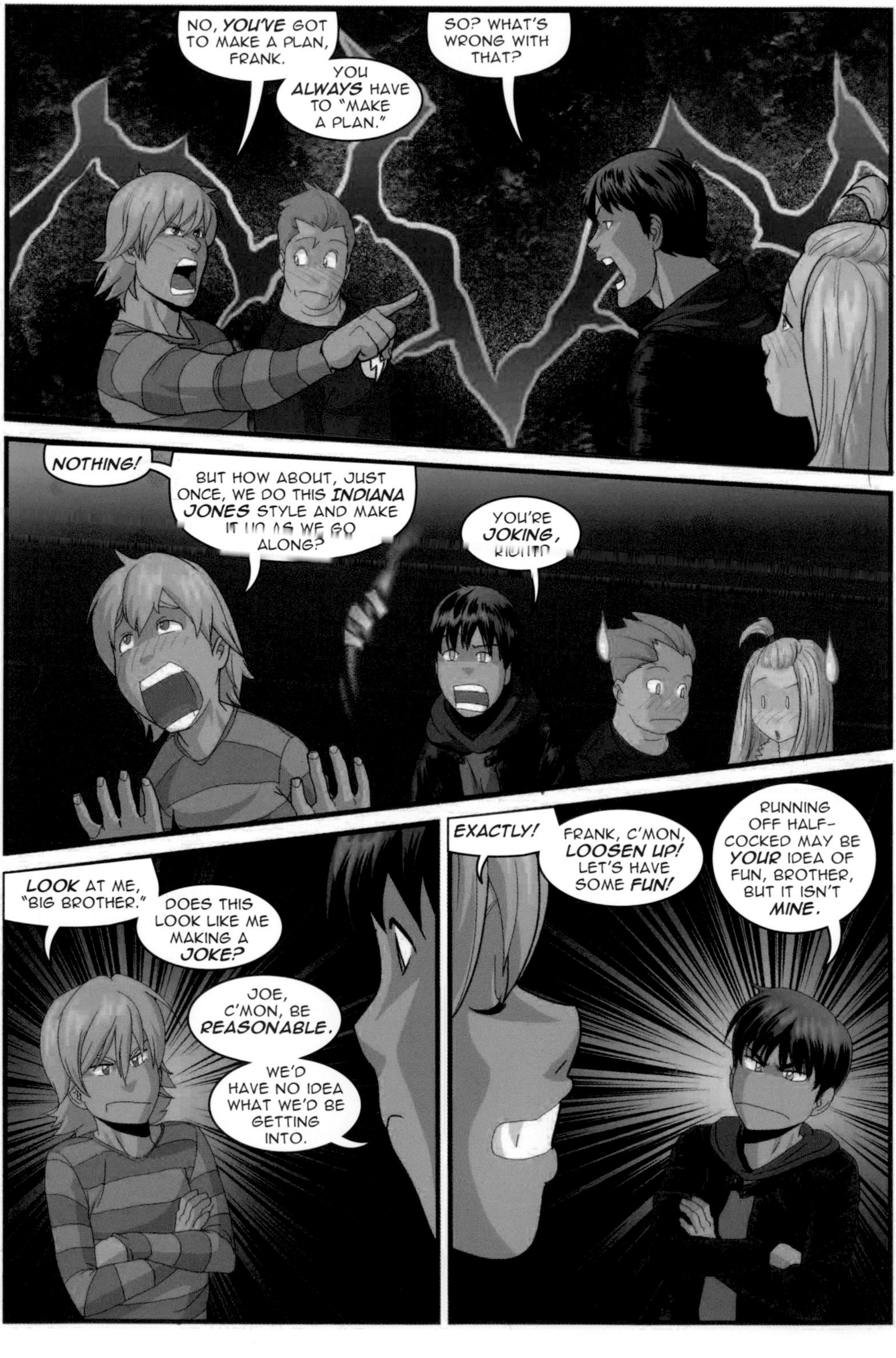
NO, *YOU'VE* GOT TO MAKE A PLAN, FRANK.
YOU *ALWAYS* HAVE TO "MAKE A PLAN."
SO? WHAT'S WRONG WITH THAT?
NOTHING!
BUT HOW ABOUT, JUST ONCE, WE DO THIS *INDIANA JONES* STYLE AND MAKE IT UP AS WE GO ALONG?
YOU'RE *JOKING,*
LOOK AT ME, "BIG BROTHER."
DOES THIS LOOK LIKE ME MAKING A *JOKE?*
JOE, C'MON, BE *REASONABLE.*
WE'D HAVE NO IDEA WHAT WE'D BE GETTING INTO.
EXACTLY!
FRANK, C'MON, *LOOSEN UP!* LET'S HAVE SOME *FUN!*
RUNNING OFF HALF-COCKED MAY BE *YOUR* IDEA OF FUN, BROTHER, BUT IT ISN'T *MINE.*

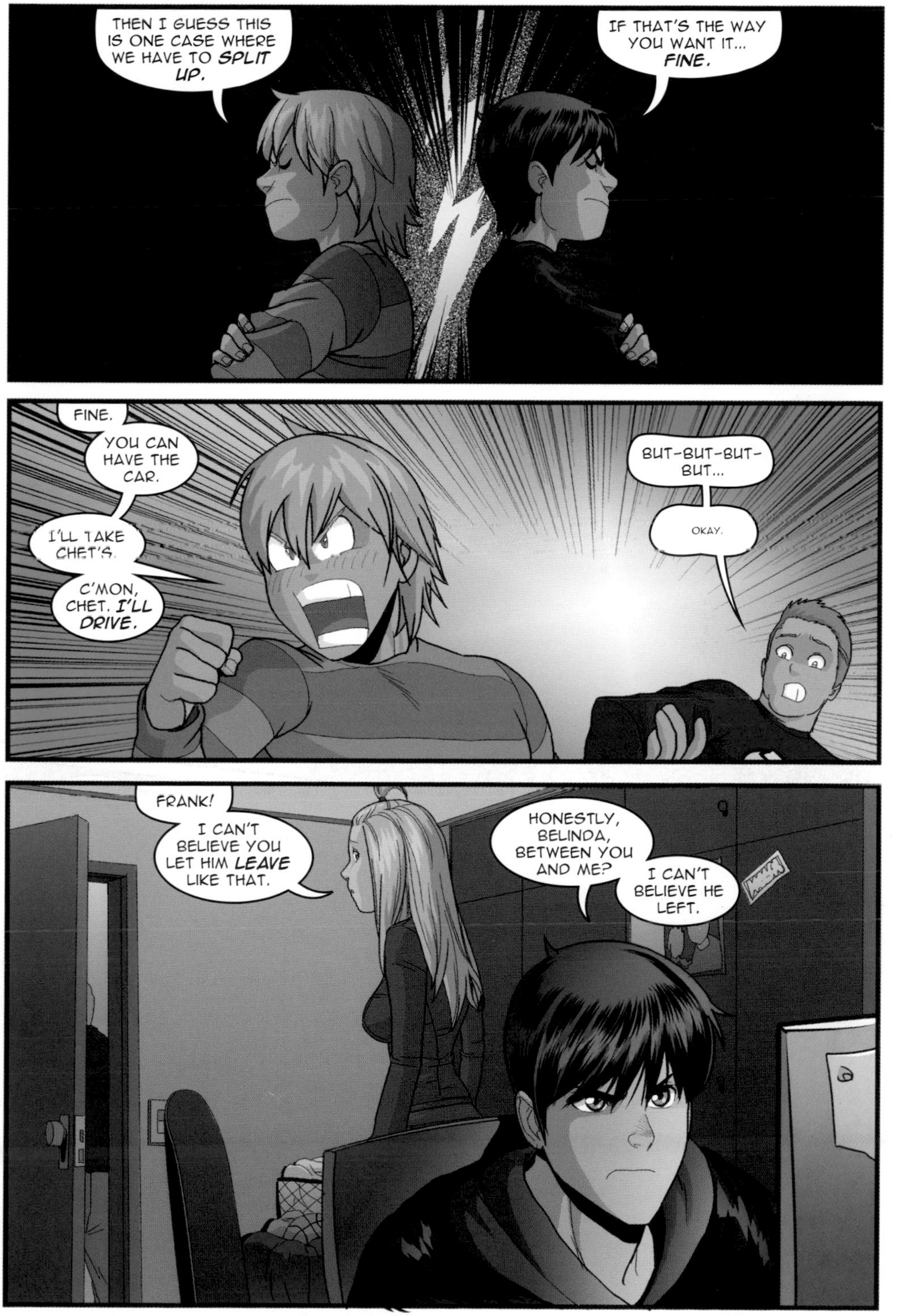
THEN I GUESS THIS IS ONE CASE WHERE WE HAVE TO SPLIT UP.
IF THAT'S THE WAY YOU WANT IT... FINE.
FINE.
YOU CAN HAVE THE CAR.
I'LL TAKE CHET'S.
C'MON, CHET. I'LL DRIVE.
BUT-BUT-BUT-BUT...
OKAY.
FRANK!
I CAN'T BELIEVE YOU LET HIM LEAVE LIKE THAT.
HONESTLY, BELINDA, BETWEEN YOU AND ME?
I CAN'T BELIEVE HE LEFT.

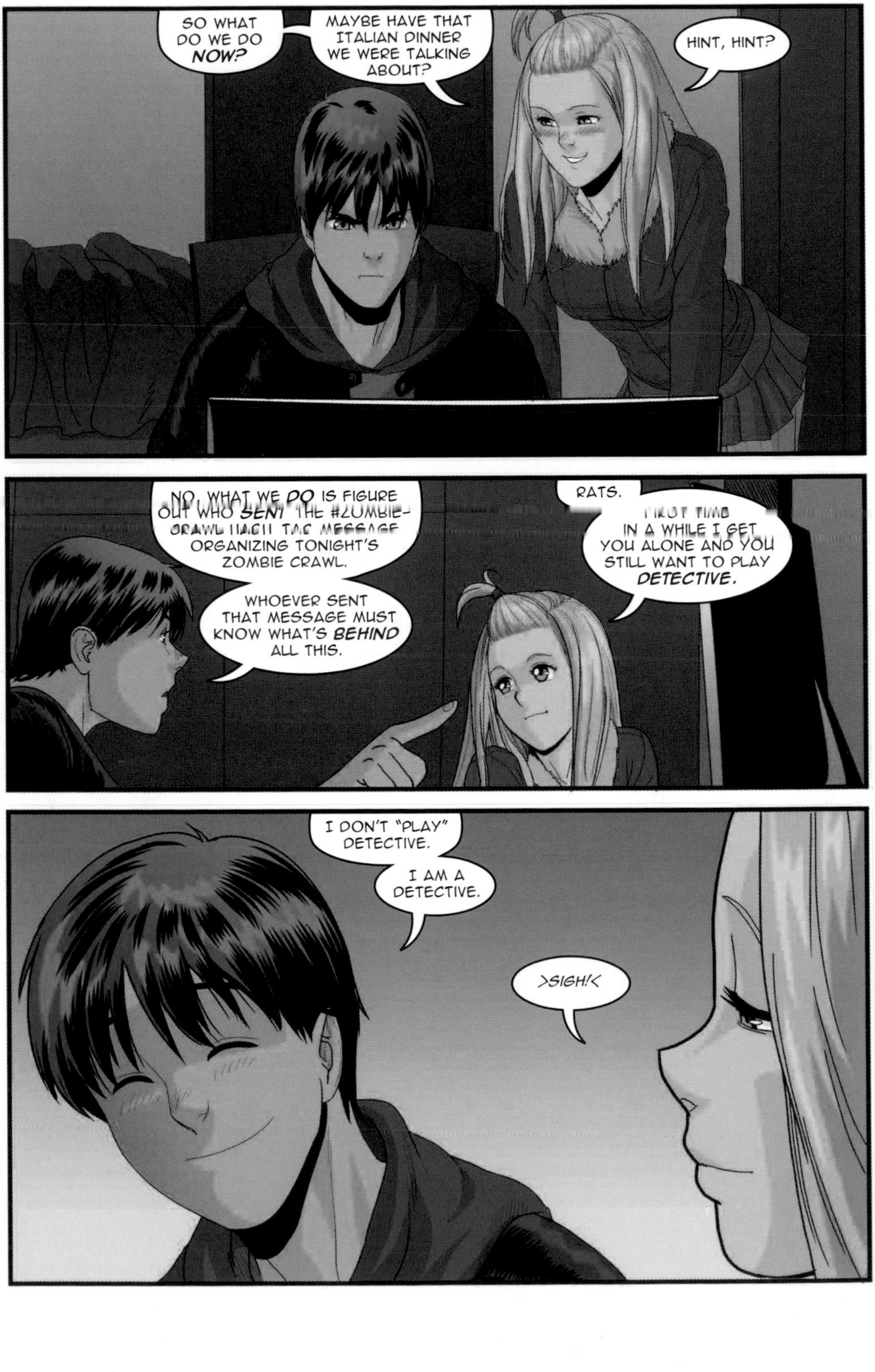
SO WHAT DO WE DO *NOW?*
MAYBE HAVE THAT ITALIAN DINNER WE WERE TALKING ABOUT?
HINT, HINT?
NO, WHAT WE *DO* IS FIGURE OUT WHO *SENT* THE #ZOMBIE-CRAWL HASH TAG MESSAGE ORGANIZING TONIGHT'S ZOMBIE CRAWL.
WHOEVER SENT THAT MESSAGE MUST KNOW WHAT'S *BEHIND* ALL THIS.
RATS.
FIRST TIME IN A WHILE I GET YOU ALONE AND YOU STILL WANT TO PLAY *DETECTIVE.*
I DON'T "PLAY" DETECTIVE.
I AM A DETECTIVE.
>SIGH!<

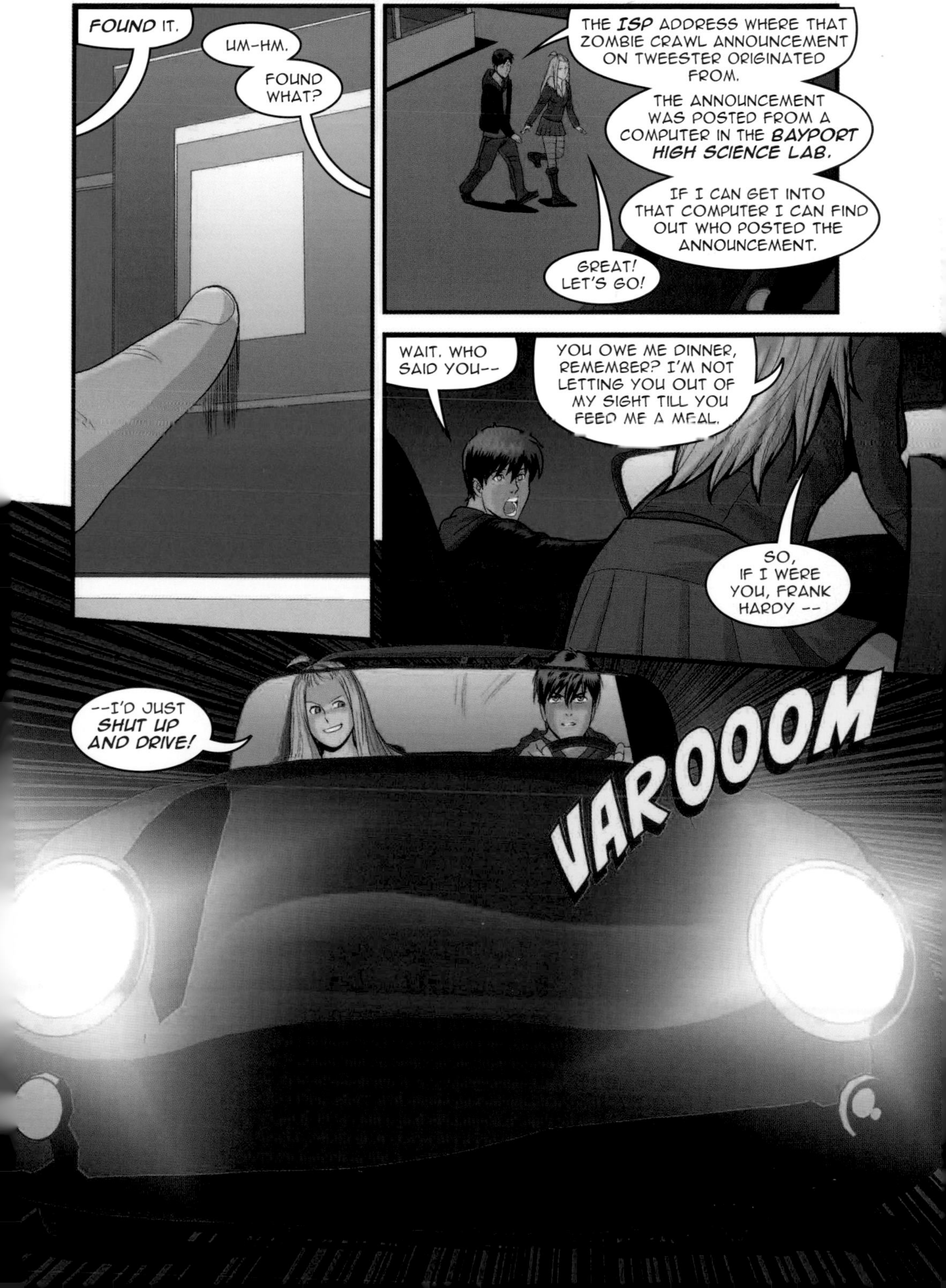
FOUND IT.
UM-HM.
FOUND WHAT?
THE ISP ADDRESS WHERE THAT ZOMBIE CRAWL ANNOUNCEMENT ON TWEESTER ORIGINATED FROM.
THE ANNOUNCEMENT WAS POSTED FROM A COMPUTER IN THE BAYPORT HIGH SCIENCE LAB.
IF I CAN GET INTO THAT COMPUTER I CAN FIND OUT WHO POSTED THE ANNOUNCEMENT.
GREAT! LET'S GO!
WAIT. WHO SAID YOU--
YOU OWE ME DINNER, REMEMBER? I'M NOT LETTING YOU OUT OF MY SIGHT TILL YOU FEED ME A MEAL.
SO, IF I WERE YOU, FRANK HARDY --
--I'D JUST SHUT UP AND DRIVE!
VAROOOM

CHAPTER FOUR: THEIR CHEMICAL ROMANCE

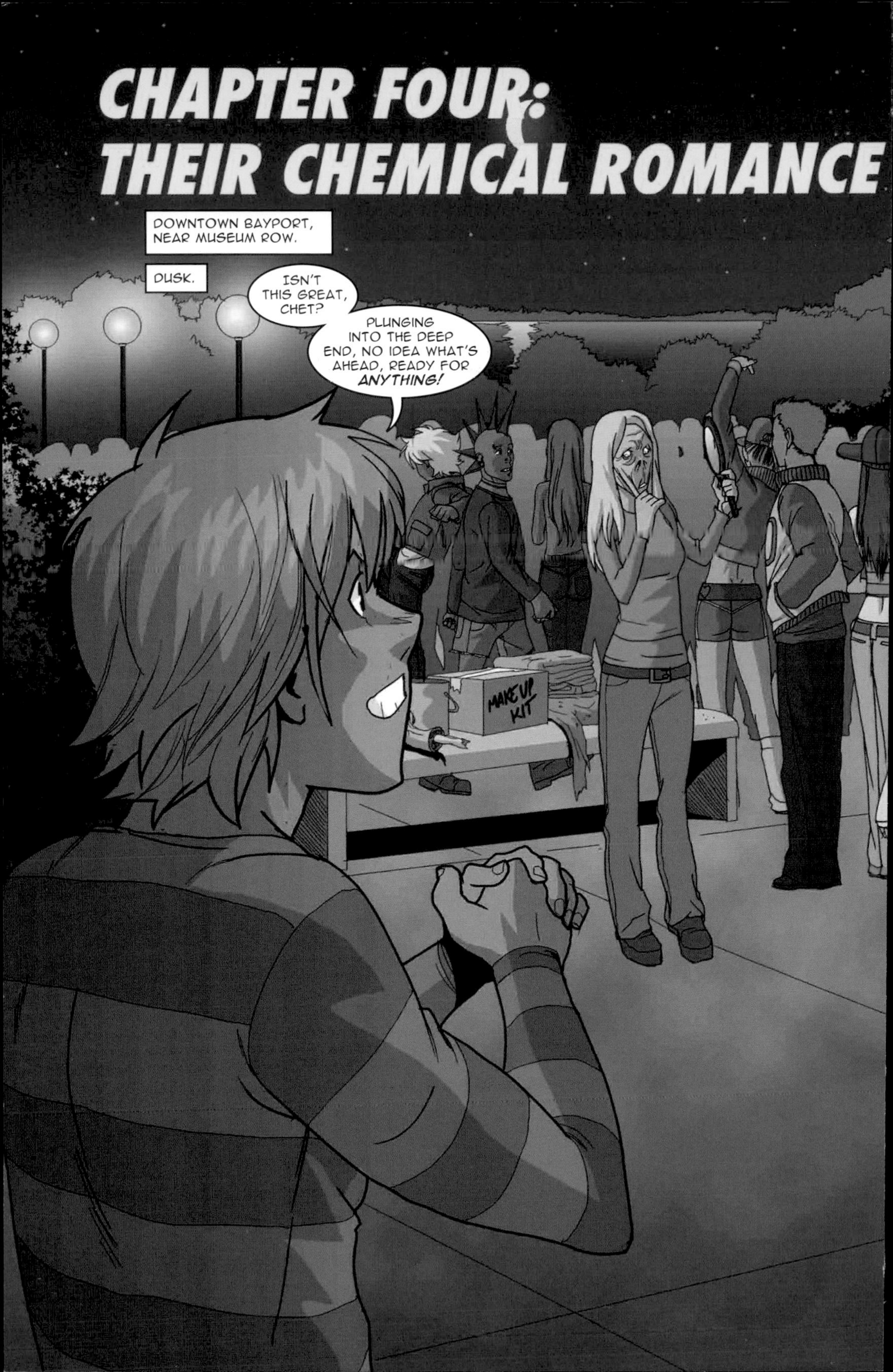
DOWNTOWN BAYPORT, NEAR MUSEUM ROW.
DUSK.
ISN'T THIS GREAT, CHET?
PLUNGING INTO THE DEEP END, NO IDEA WHAT'S AHEAD, READY FOR *ANYTHING!*
MAKE UP KIT

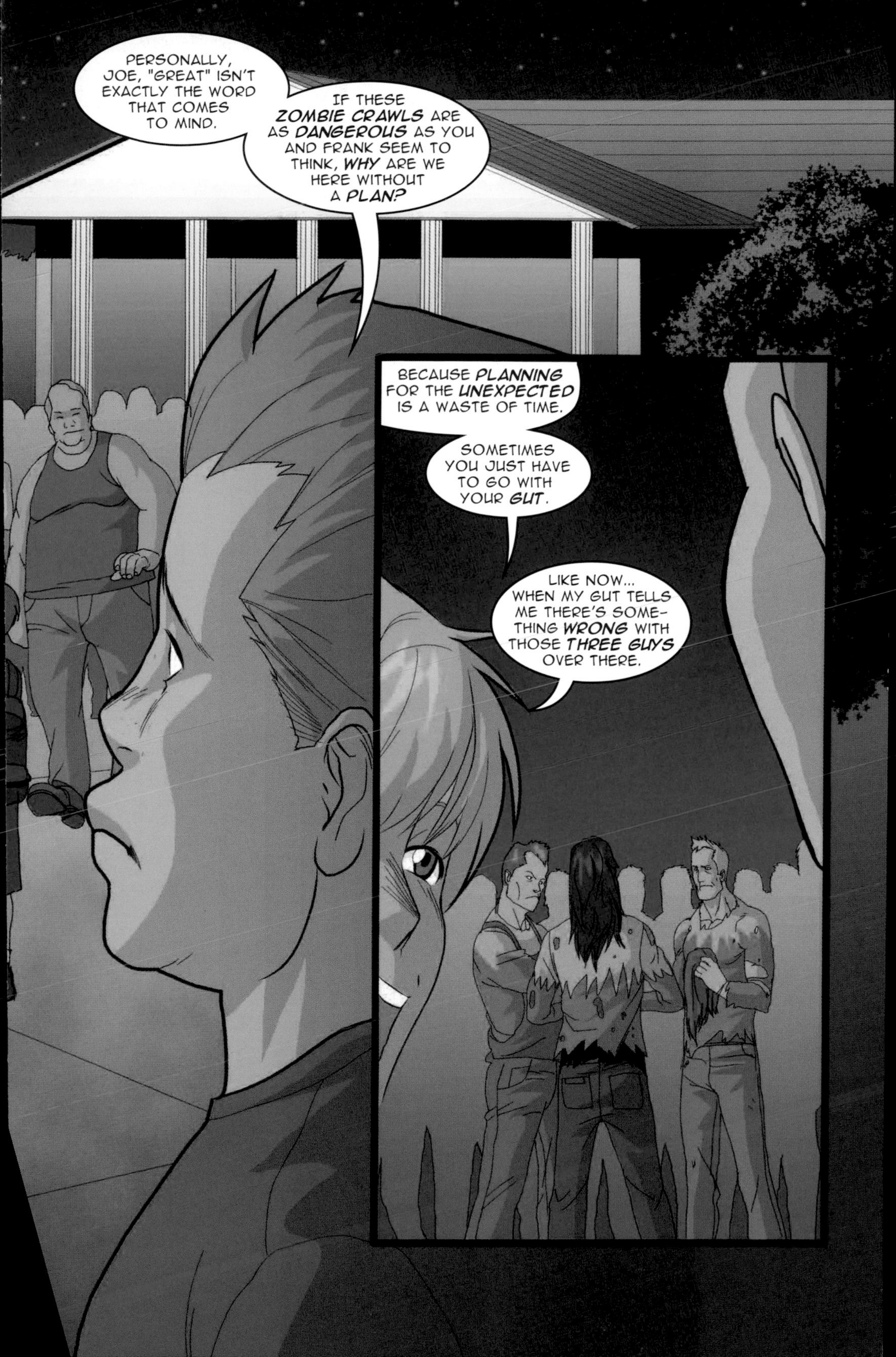
PERSONALLY, JOE, "GREAT" ISN'T EXACTLY THE WORD THAT COMES TO MIND.
IF THESE ZOMBIE CRAWLS ARE AS DANGEROUS AS YOU AND FRANK SEEM TO THINK, WHY ARE WE HERE WITHOUT A PLAN?
BECAUSE PLANNING FOR THE UNEXPECTED IS A WASTE OF TIME.
SOMETIMES YOU JUST HAVE TO GO WITH YOUR GUT.
LIKE NOW... WHEN MY GUT TELLS ME THERE'S SOME-THING WRONG WITH THOSE THREE GUYS OVER THERE.

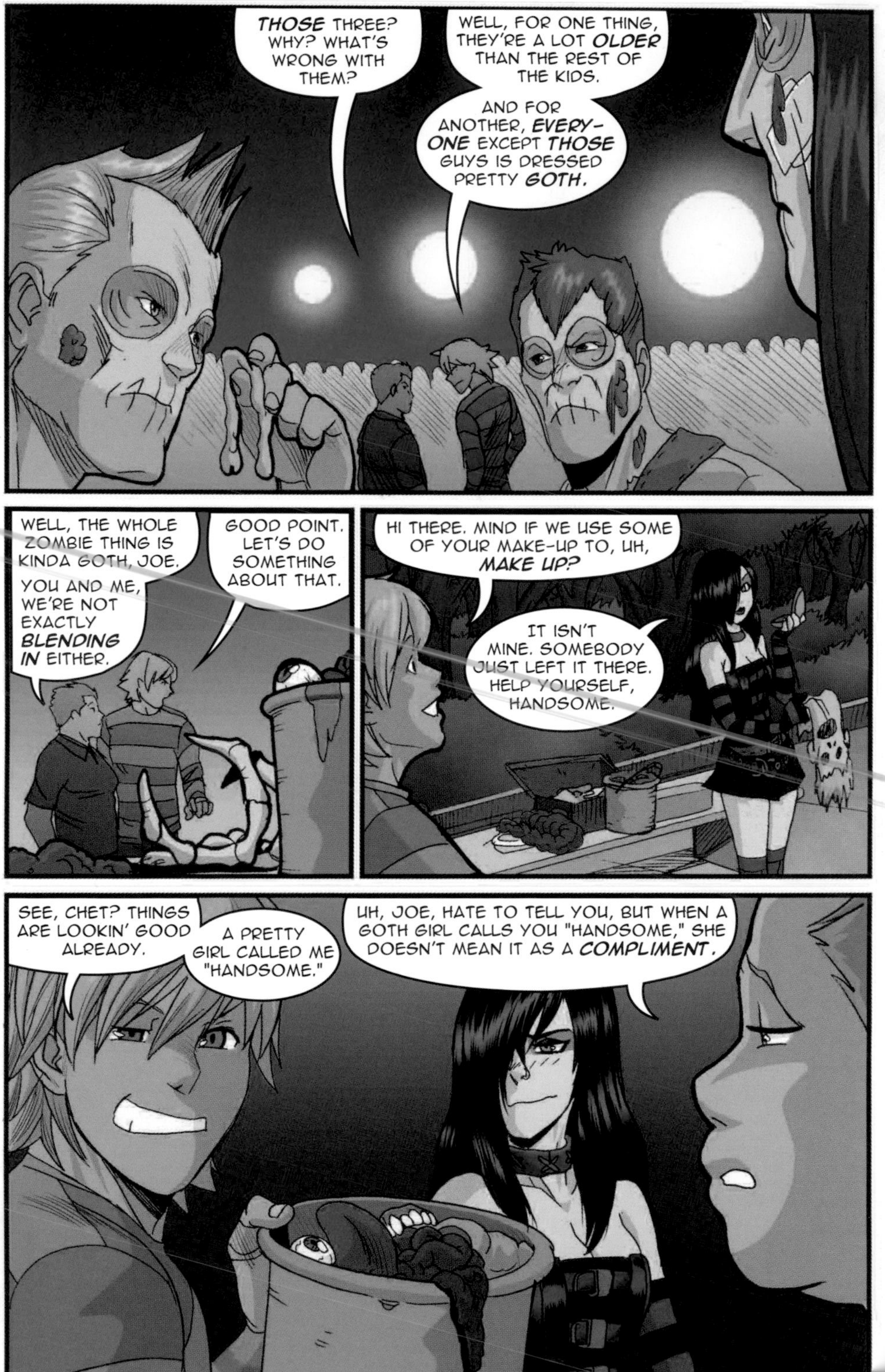
THOSE THREE? WHY? WHAT'S WRONG WITH THEM?
WELL, FOR ONE THING, THEY'RE A LOT OLDER THAN THE REST OF THE KIDS.
AND FOR ANOTHER, EVERY-ONE EXCEPT THOSE GUYS IS DRESSED PRETTY GOTH.
WELL, THE WHOLE ZOMBIE THING IS KINDA GOTH, JOE.
YOU AND ME, WE'RE NOT EXACTLY BLENDING IN EITHER.
GOOD POINT. LET'S DO SOMETHING ABOUT THAT.
HI THERE. MIND IF WE USE SOME OF YOUR MAKE-UP TO, UH, MAKE UP?
IT ISN'T MINE. SOMEBODY JUST LEFT IT THERE. HELP YOURSELF, HANDSOME.
SEE, CHET? THINGS ARE LOOKIN' GOOD ALREADY.
A PRETTY GIRL CALLED ME "HANDSOME."
UH, JOE, HATE TO TELL YOU, BUT WHEN A GOTH GIRL CALLS YOU "HANDSOME," SHE DOESN'T MEAN IT AS A COMPLIMENT.

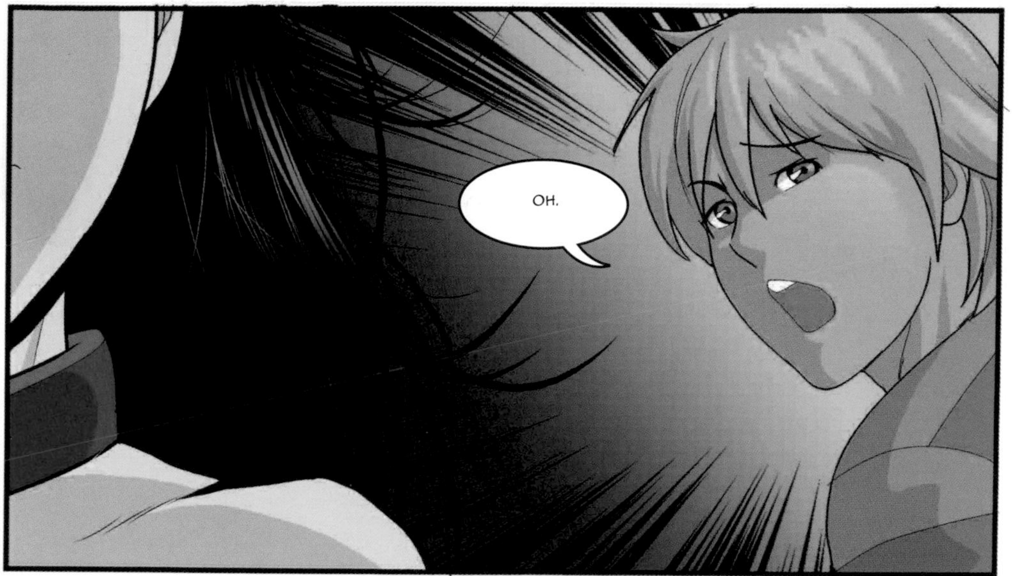
OH.

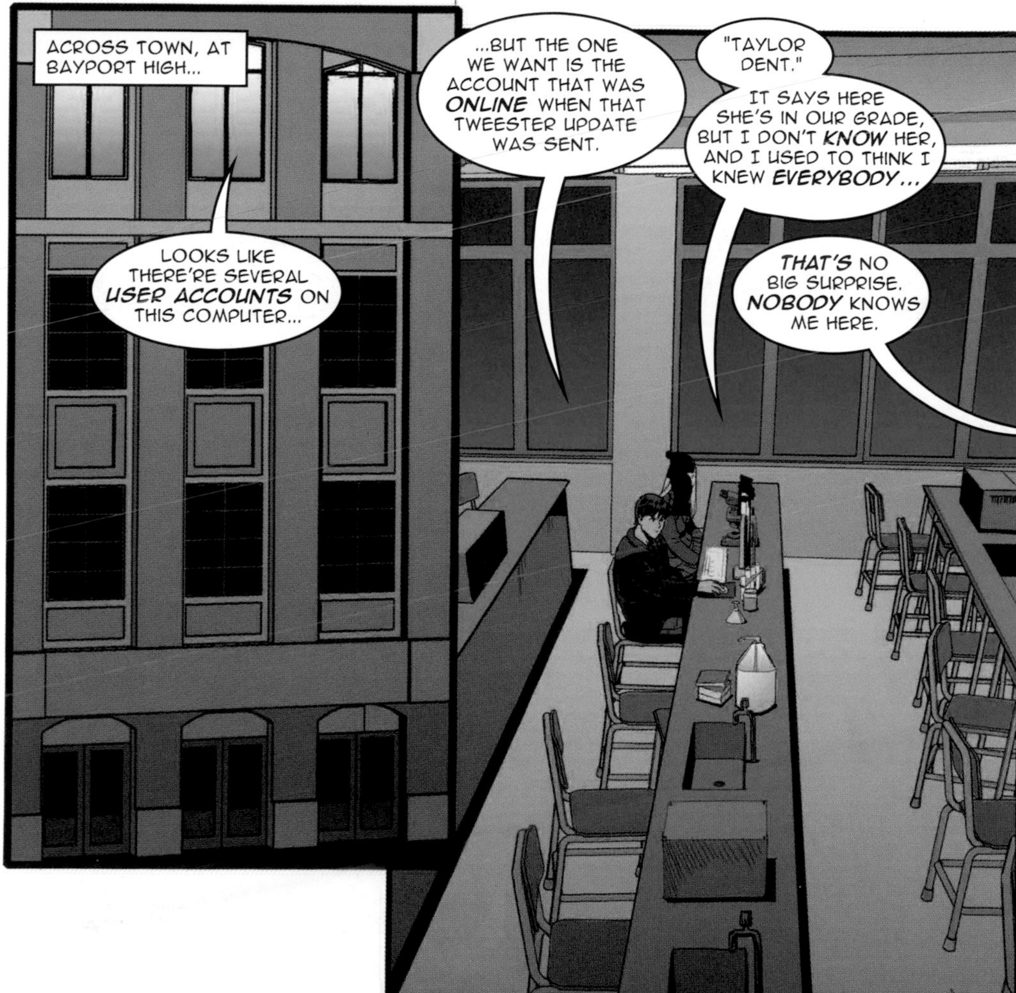
ACROSS TOWN, AT BAYPORT HIGH...
LOOKS LIKE THERE'RE SEVERAL USER ACCOUNTS ON THIS COMPUTER...
...BUT THE ONE WE WANT IS THE ACCOUNT THAT WAS ONLINE WHEN THAT TWEESTER UPDATE WAS SENT.
"TAYLOR DENT."
IT SAYS HERE SHE'S IN OUR GRADE, BUT I DON'T KNOW HER, AND I USED TO THINK I KNEW EVERYBODY...
THAT'S NO BIG SURPRISE. NOBODY KNOWS ME HERE.

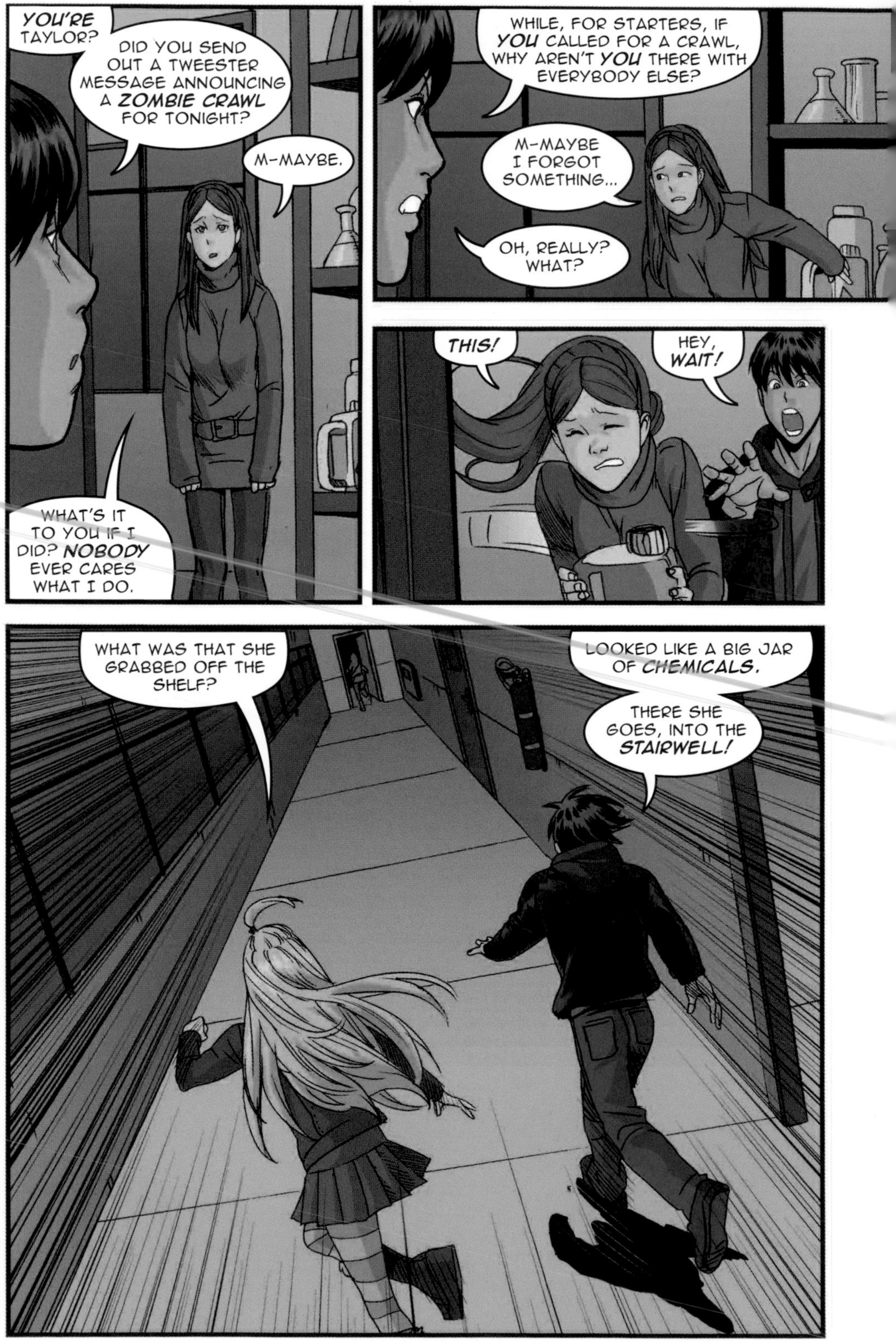
YOU'RE TAYLOR?
DID YOU SEND OUT A TWEESTER MESSAGE ANNOUNCING A ZOMBIE CRAWL FOR TONIGHT?
M-MAYBE.
WHAT'S IT TO YOU IF I DID? NOBODY EVER CARES WHAT I DO.
WHILE, FOR STARTERS, IF YOU CALLED FOR A CRAWL, WHY AREN'T YOU THERE WITH EVERYBODY ELSE?
M-MAYBE I FORGOT SOMETHING...
OH, REALLY? WHAT?
THIS!
HEY, WAIT!
WHAT WAS THAT SHE GRABBED OFF THE SHELF?
LOOKED LIKE A BIG JAR OF CHEMICALS.
THERE SHE GOES, INTO THE STAIRWELL!

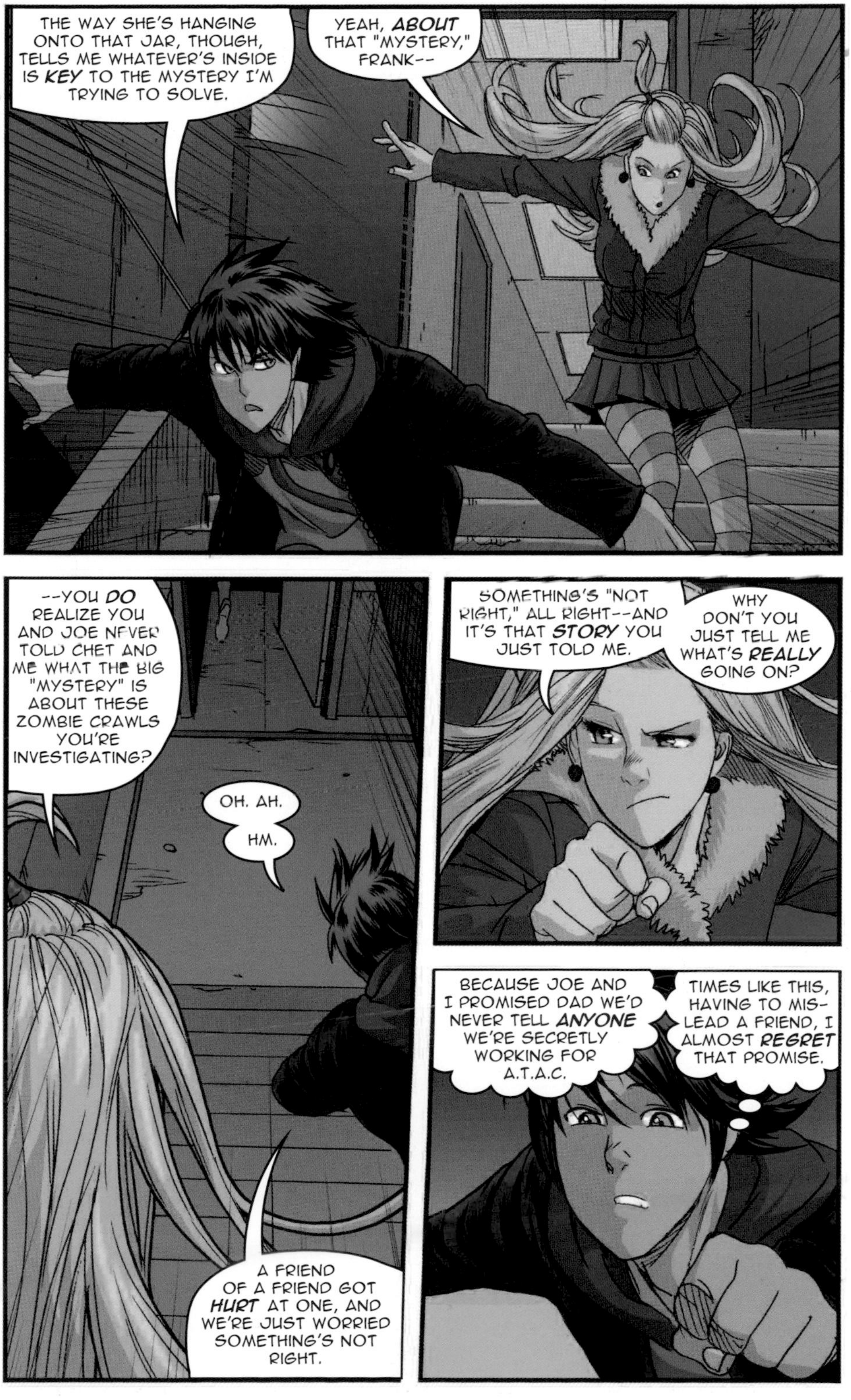
THE WAY SHE'S HANGING ONTO THAT JAR, THOUGH, TELLS ME WHATEVER'S INSIDE IS KEY TO THE MYSTERY I'M TRYING TO SOLVE.
YEAH, ABOUT THAT "MYSTERY," FRANK--
--YOU DO REALIZE YOU AND JOE NEVER TOLD CHET AND ME WHAT THE BIG "MYSTERY" IS ABOUT THESE ZOMBIE CRAWLS YOU'RE INVESTIGATING?
OH. AH.
HM.
A FRIEND OF A FRIEND GOT HURT AT ONE, AND WE'RE JUST WORRIED SOMETHING'S NOT RIGHT.
SOMETHING'S "NOT RIGHT," ALL RIGHT--AND IT'S THAT STORY YOU JUST TOLD ME.
WHY DON'T YOU JUST TELL ME WHAT'S REALLY GOING ON?
BECAUSE JOE AND I PROMISED DAD WE'D NEVER TELL ANYONE WE'RE SECRETLY WORKING FOR A.T.A.C.
TIMES LIKE THIS, HAVING TO MIS-LEAD A FRIEND, I ALMOST REGRET THAT PROMISE.

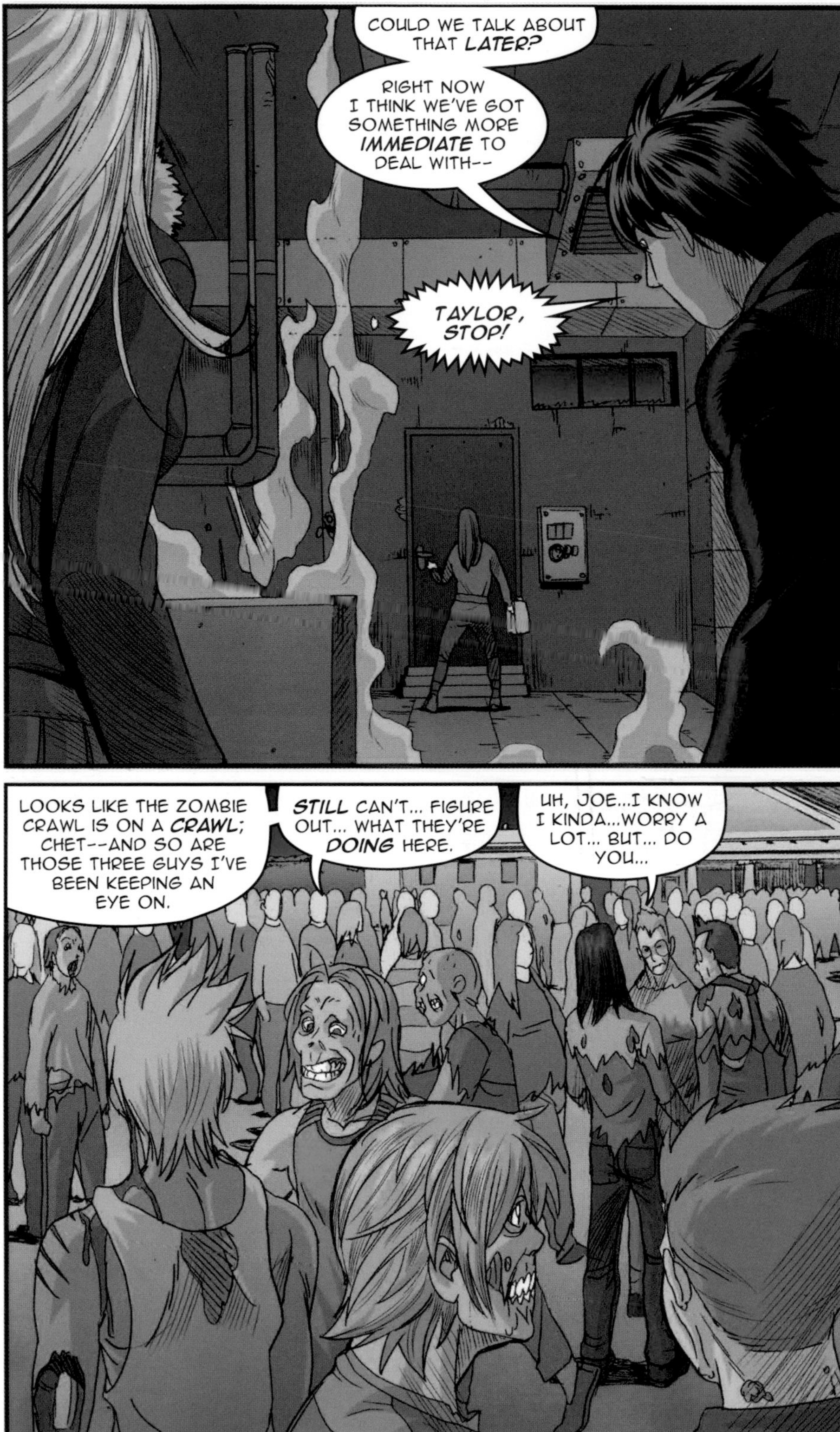
COULD WE TALK ABOUT THAT LATER?
RIGHT NOW I THINK WE'VE GOT SOMETHING MORE IMMEDIATE TO DEAL WITH--
TAYLOR, STOP!
LOOKS LIKE THE ZOMBIE CRAWL IS ON A CRAWL; CHET--AND SO ARE THOSE THREE GUYS I'VE BEEN KEEPING AN EYE ON.
STILL CAN'T... FIGURE OUT... WHAT THEY'RE DOING HERE.
UH, JOE...I KNOW I KINDA...WORRY A LOT... BUT... DO YOU...

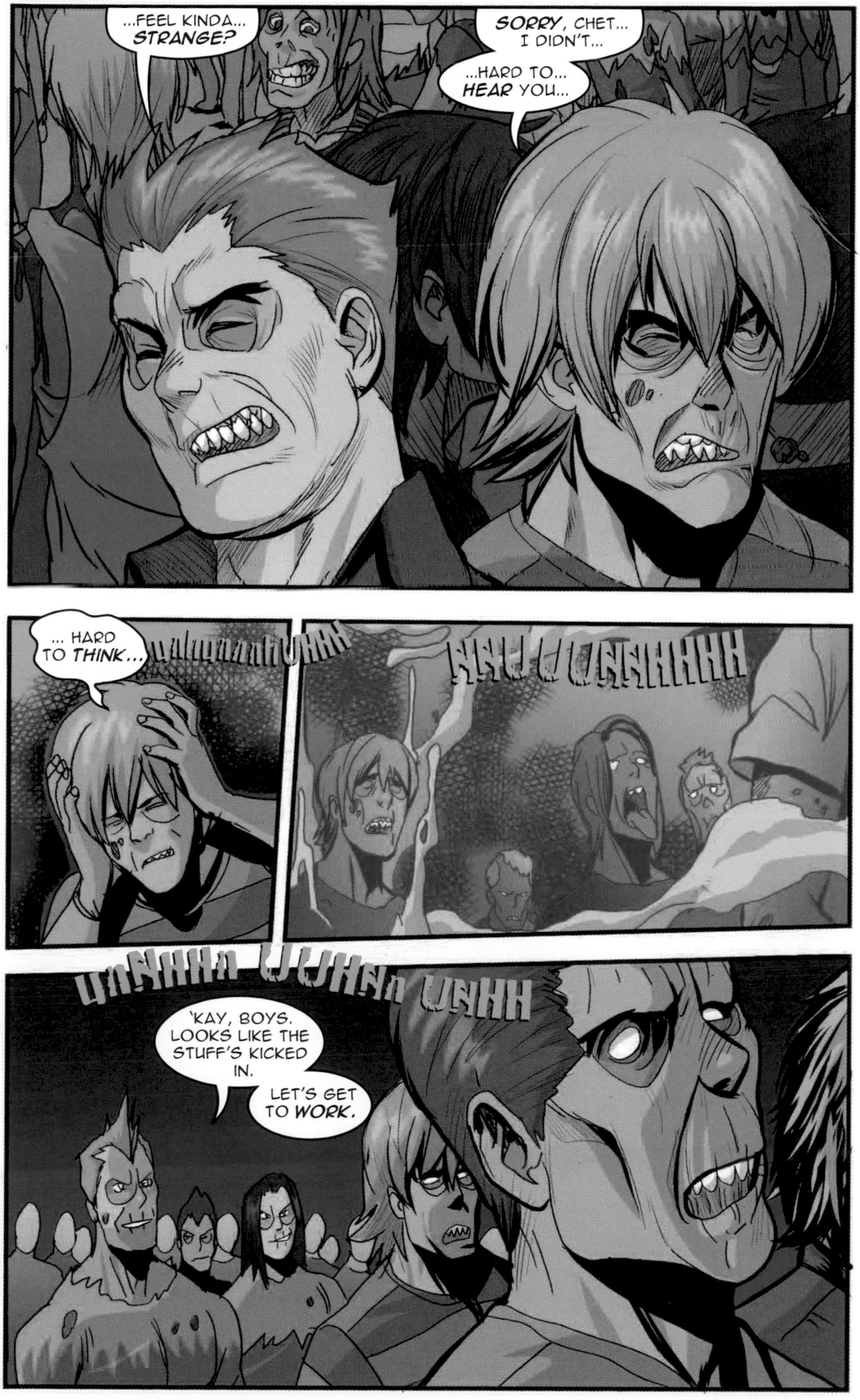

...FEEL KINDA... **STRANGE?**
SORRY, CHET... I DIDN'T...
...HARD TO... **HEAR** YOU...
... HARD TO **THINK**...
'KAY, BOYS. LOOKS LIKE THE STUFF'S KICKED IN.
LET'S GET TO **WORK.**

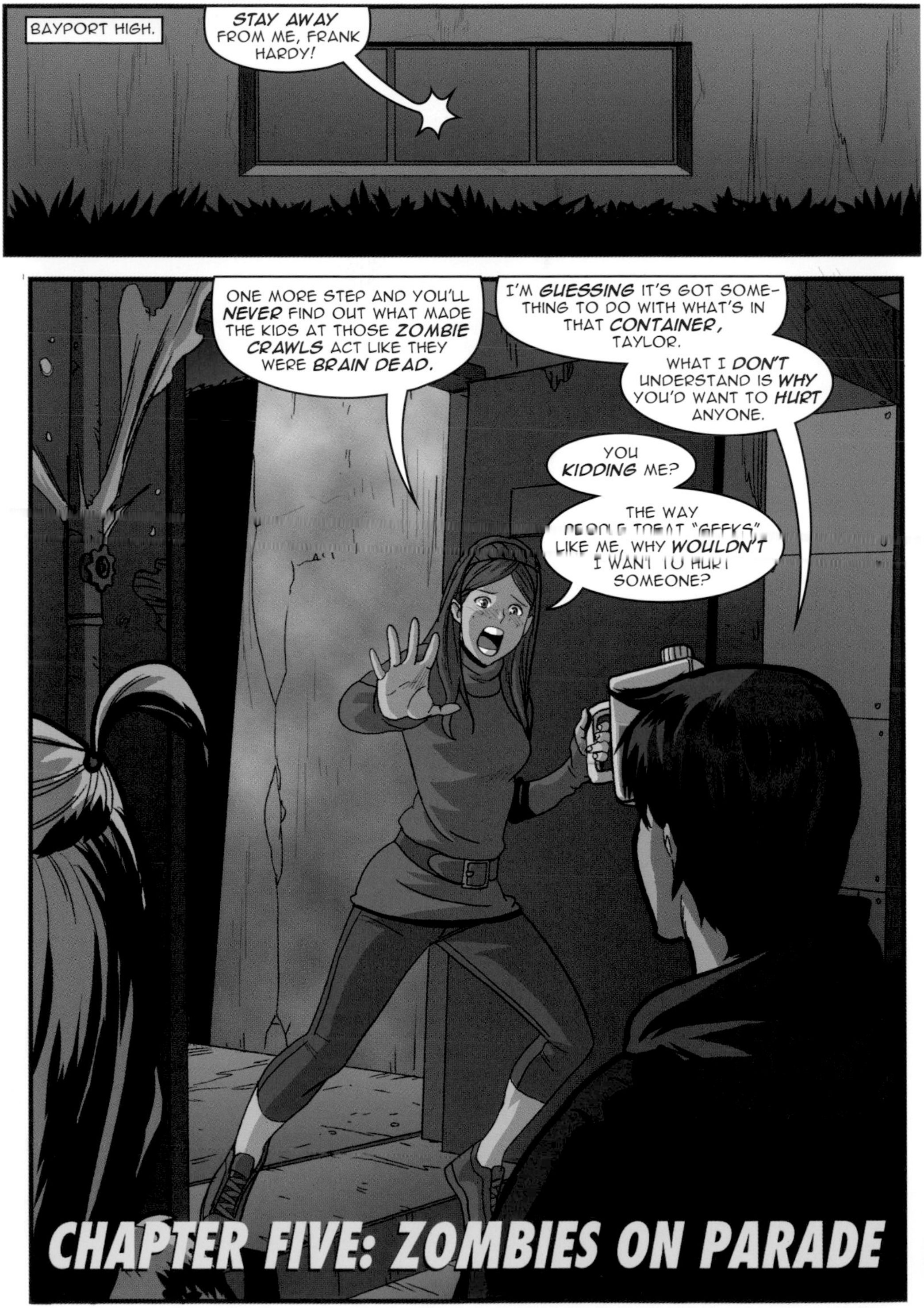
BAYPORT HIGH.
STAY AWAY FROM ME, FRANK HARDY!
ONE MORE STEP AND YOU'LL NEVER FIND OUT WHAT MADE THE KIDS AT THOSE ZOMBIE CRAWLS ACT LIKE THEY WERE BRAIN DEAD.
I'M GUESSING IT'S GOT SOMETHING TO DO WITH WHAT'S IN THAT CONTAINER, TAYLOR.
WHAT I DON'T UNDERSTAND IS WHY YOU'D WANT TO HURT ANYONE.
YOU KIDDING ME?
THE WAY PEOPLE TREAT "GEEKS" LIKE ME, WHY WOULDN'T I WANT TO HURT SOMEONE?
CHAPTER FIVE: ZOMBIES ON PARADE

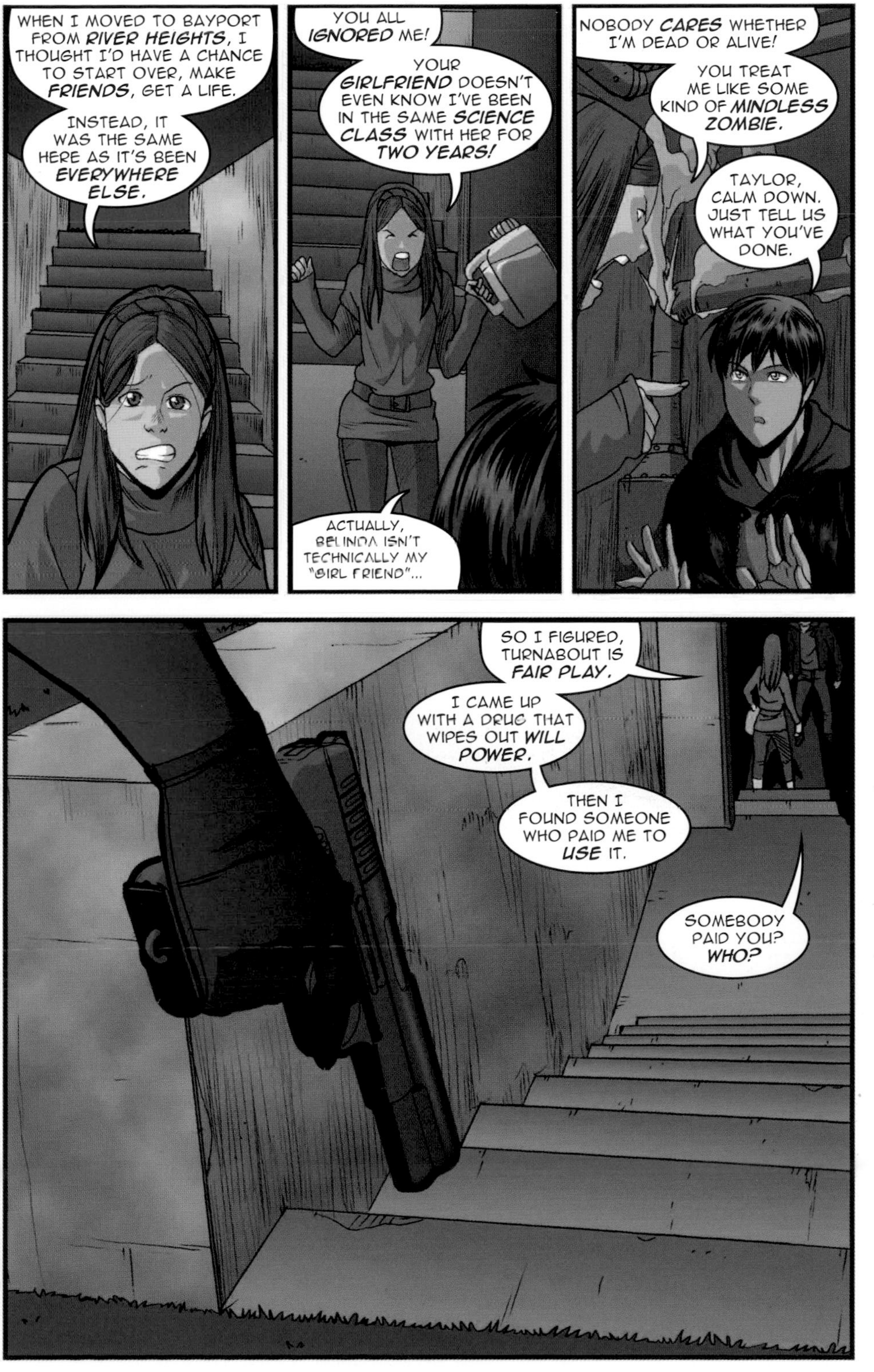
WHEN I MOVED TO BAYPORT FROM RIVER HEIGHTS, I THOUGHT I'D HAVE A CHANCE TO START OVER, MAKE FRIENDS, GET A LIFE.
INSTEAD, IT WAS THE SAME HERE AS IT'S BEEN EVERYWHERE ELSE.
YOU ALL IGNORED ME!
YOUR GIRLFRIEND DOESN'T EVEN KNOW I'VE BEEN IN THE SAME SCIENCE CLASS WITH HER FOR TWO YEARS!
ACTUALLY, BELINDA ISN'T TECHNICALLY MY "GIRL FRIEND"...
NOBODY CARES WHETHER I'M DEAD OR ALIVE!
YOU TREAT ME LIKE SOME KIND OF MINDLESS ZOMBIE.
TAYLOR, CALM DOWN. JUST TELL US WHAT YOU'VE DONE.
SO I FIGURED, TURNABOUT IS FAIR PLAY.
I CAME UP WITH A DRUG THAT WIPES OUT WILL POWER.
THEN I FOUND SOMEONE WHO PAID ME TO USE IT.
SOMEBODY PAID YOU? WHO?

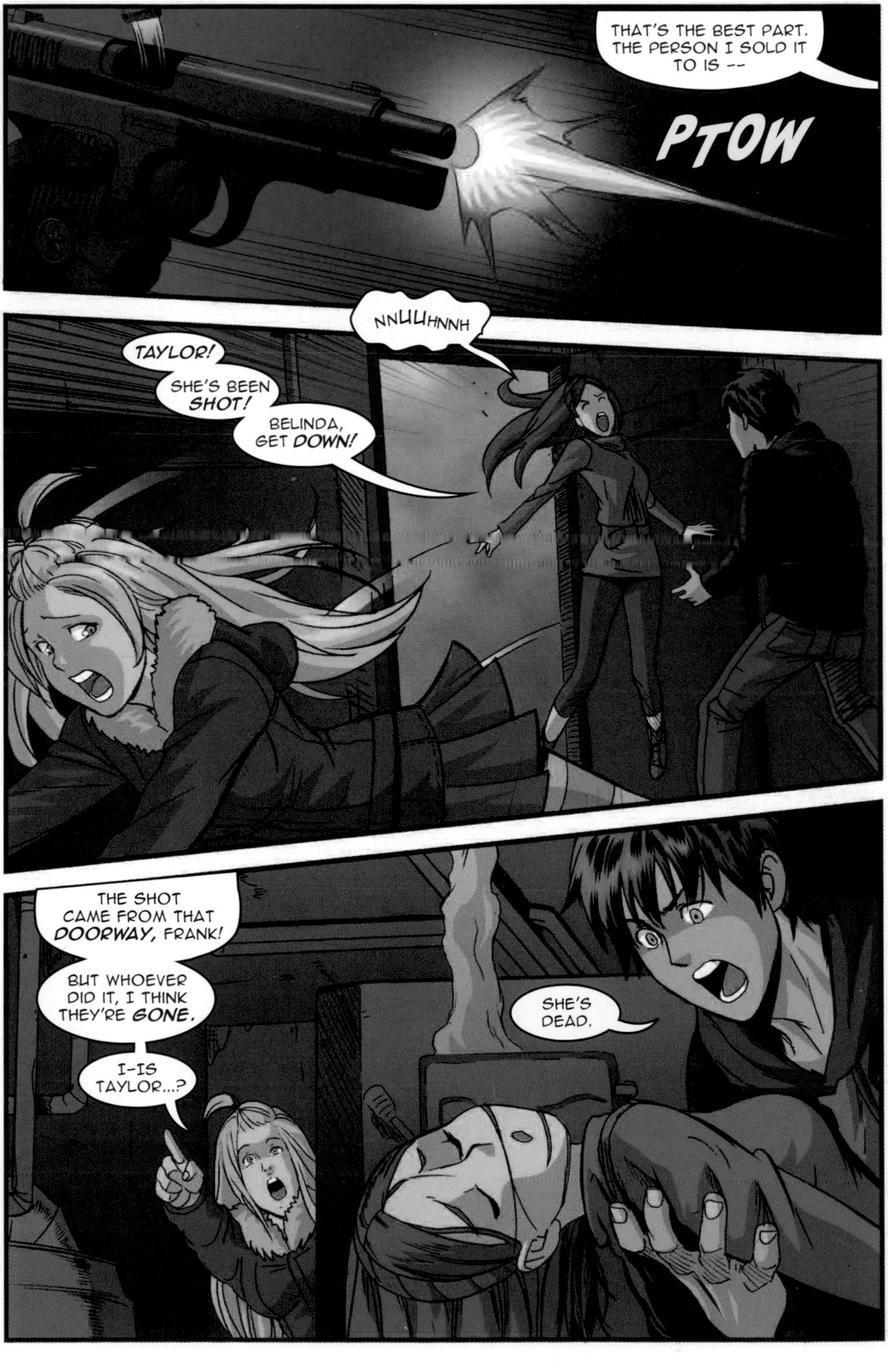
THAT'S THE BEST PART. THE PERSON I SOLD IT TO IS --
PTOW
NNUUHNNH
TAYLOR!
SHE'S BEEN SHOT!
BELINDA, GET DOWN!
THE SHOT CAME FROM THAT DOORWAY, FRANK!
BUT WHOEVER DID IT, I THINK THEY'RE GONE.
I-IS TAYLOR...?
SHE'S DEAD.

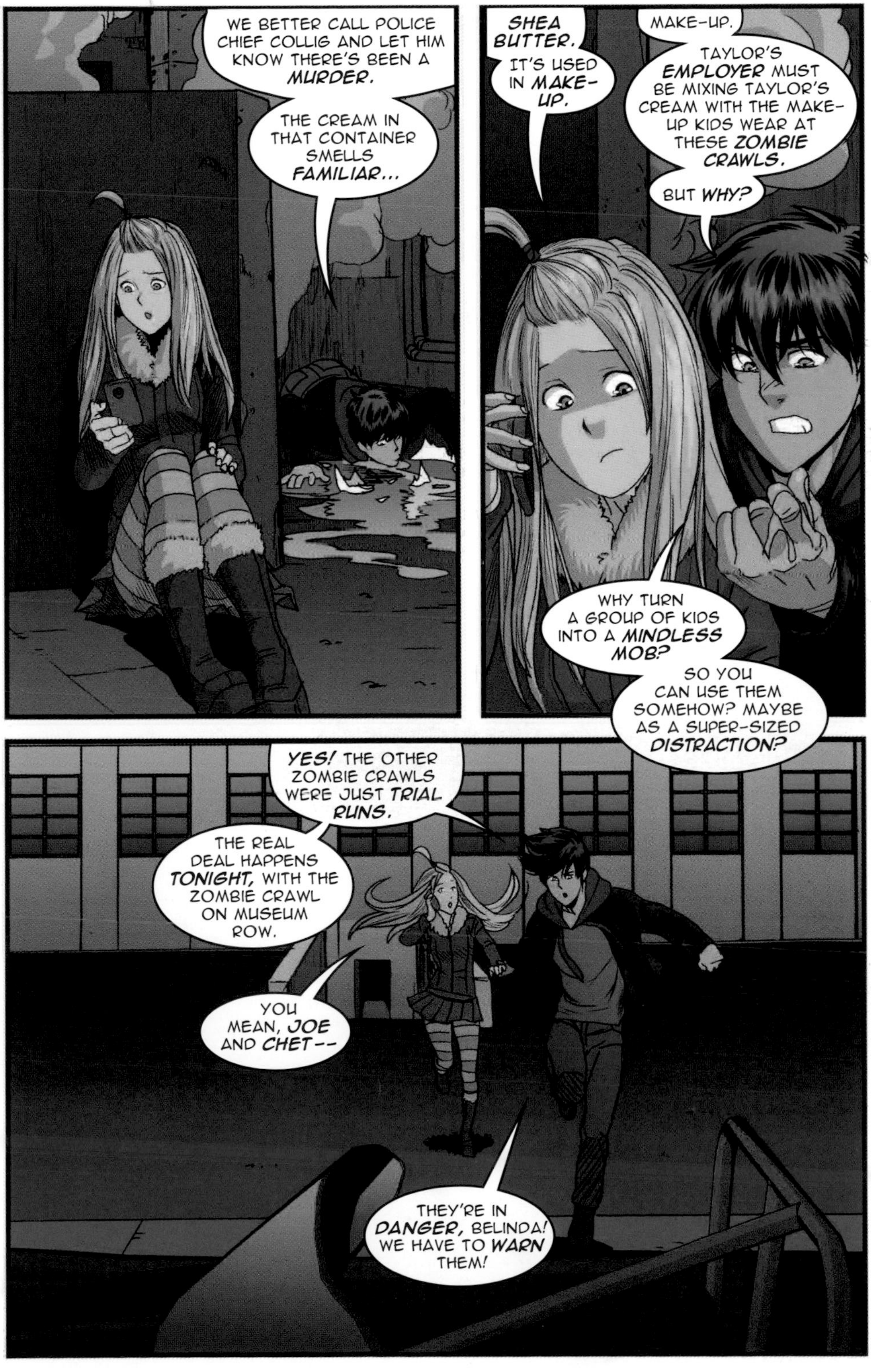

WE BETTER CALL POLICE CHIEF COLLIG AND LET HIM KNOW THERE'S BEEN A MURDER.
THE CREAM IN THAT CONTAINER SMELLS FAMILIAR...
SHEA BUTTER.
IT'S USED IN MAKE-UP.
MAKE-UP.
TAYLOR'S EMPLOYER MUST BE MIXING TAYLOR'S CREAM WITH THE MAKE-UP KIDS WEAR AT THESE ZOMBIE CRAWLS.
BUT WHY?
WHY TURN A GROUP OF KIDS INTO A MINDLESS MOB?
SO YOU CAN USE THEM SOMEHOW? MAYBE AS A SUPER-SIZED DISTRACTION?
YES! THE OTHER ZOMBIE CRAWLS WERE JUST TRIAL RUNS.
THE REAL DEAL HAPPENS TONIGHT, WITH THE ZOMBIE CRAWL ON MUSEUM ROW.
YOU MEAN, JOE AND CHET--
THEY'RE IN DANGER, BELINDA! WE HAVE TO WARN THEM!

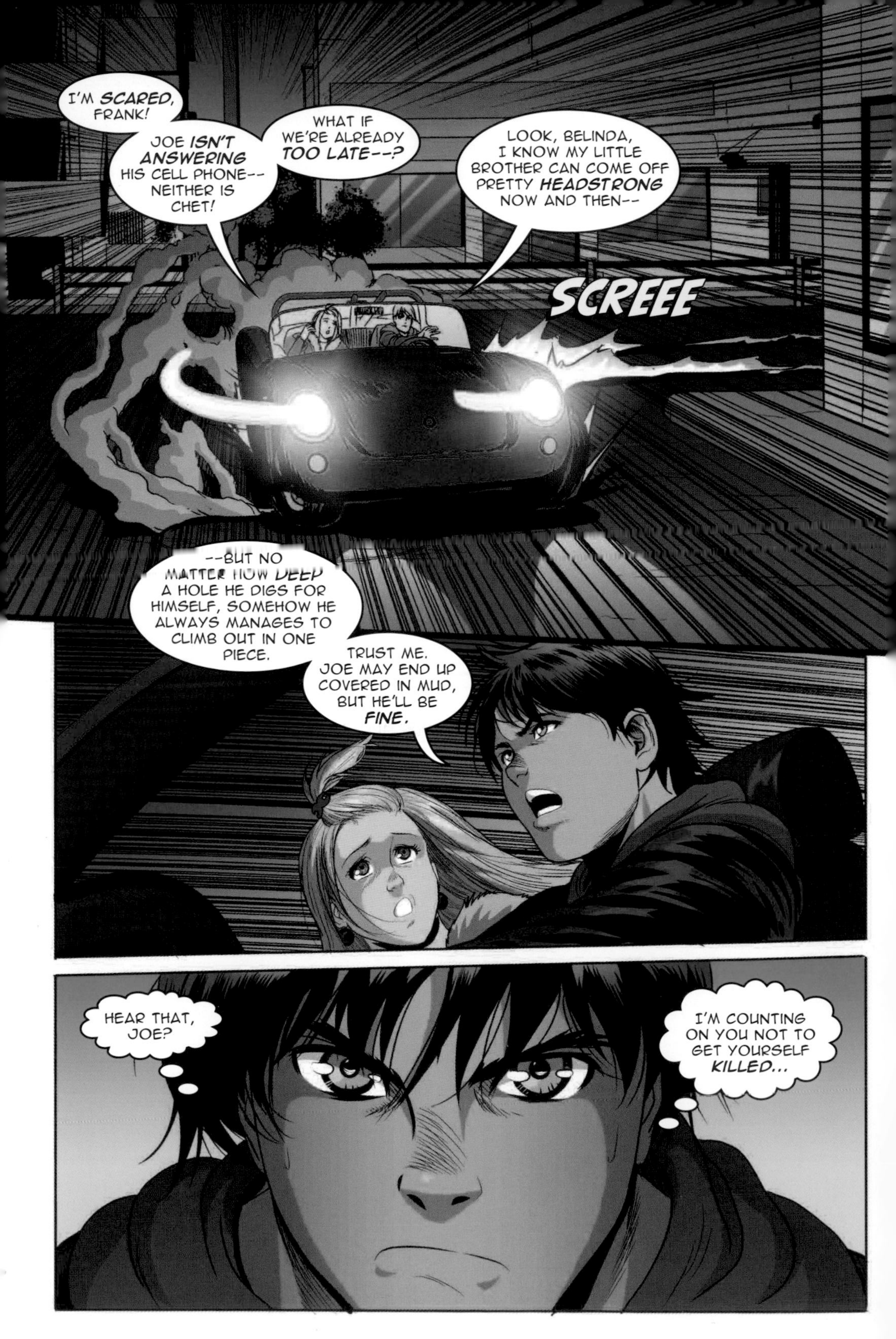
I'M SCARED, FRANK!
JOE ISN'T ANSWERING HIS CELL PHONE-- NEITHER IS CHET!
WHAT IF WE'RE ALREADY TOO LATE--?
LOOK, BELINDA, I KNOW MY LITTLE BROTHER CAN COME OFF PRETTY HEADSTRONG NOW AND THEN--
SCREEE
--BUT NO MATTER HOW DEEP A HOLE HE DIGS FOR HIMSELF, SOMEHOW HE ALWAYS MANAGES TO CLIMB OUT IN ONE PIECE.
TRUST ME. JOE MAY END UP COVERED IN MUD, BUT HE'LL BE FINE.
HEAR THAT, JOE?
I'M COUNTING ON YOU NOT TO GET YOURSELF KILLED...

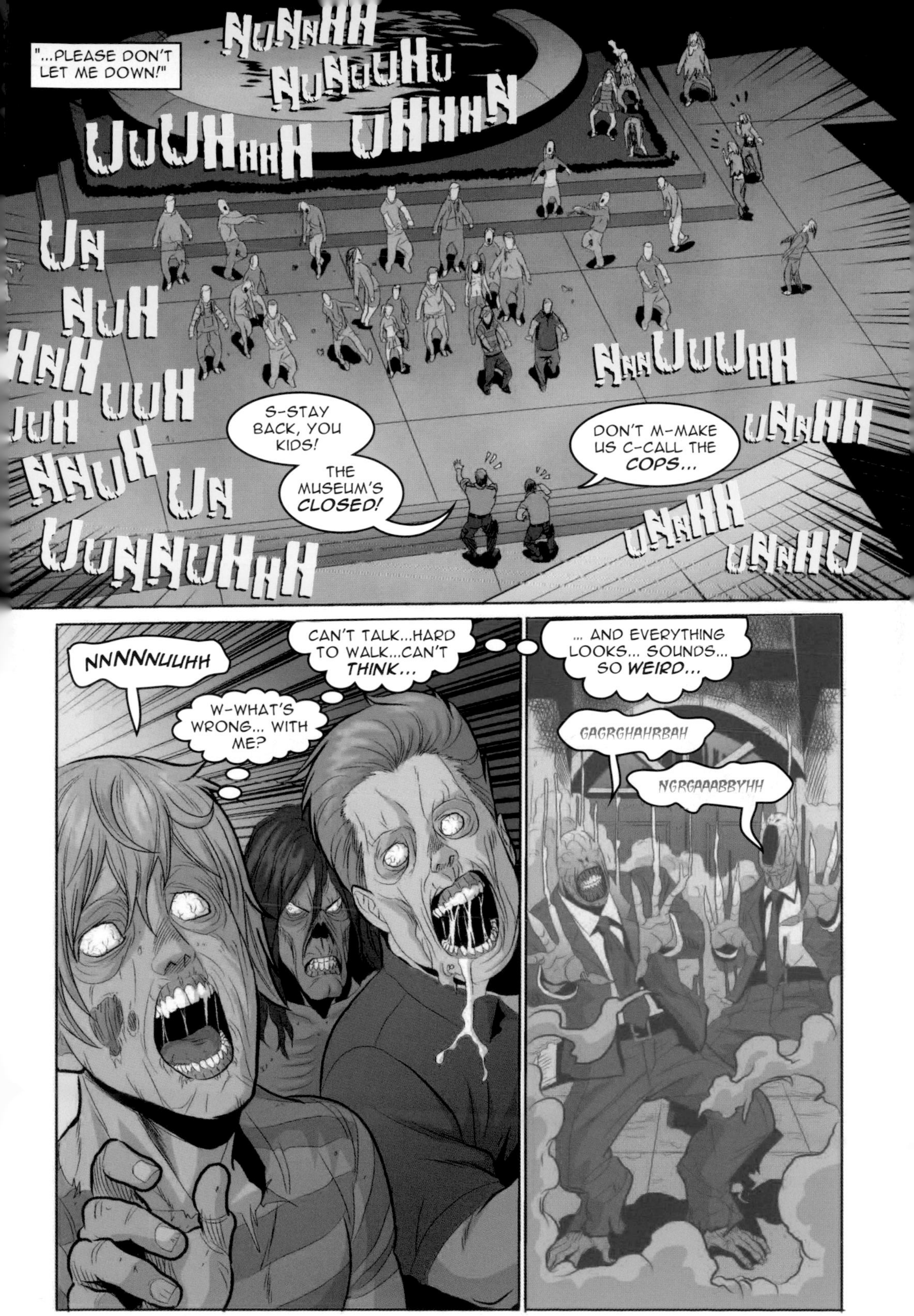
"...PLEASE DON'T LET ME DOWN!"
NUNNHH
NUNUUHU
UUUHHHH
UHHHN
UN
NUH
HNH
UUH
JUH
NNUH
UN
UUNNUHHH
NNNUUUHH
UNNHH
UNNHH
UNNHU
S-STAY BACK, YOU KIDS!
THE MUSEUM'S CLOSED!
DON'T M-MAKE US C-CALL THE COPS...
NNNNNUUHH
W-WHAT'S WRONG... WITH ME?
CAN'T TALK...HARD TO WALK...CAN'T THINK...
... AND EVERYTHING LOOKS... SOUNDS... SO WEIRD...
GAGRGHAHRBAH
NGRGAAABBYHH

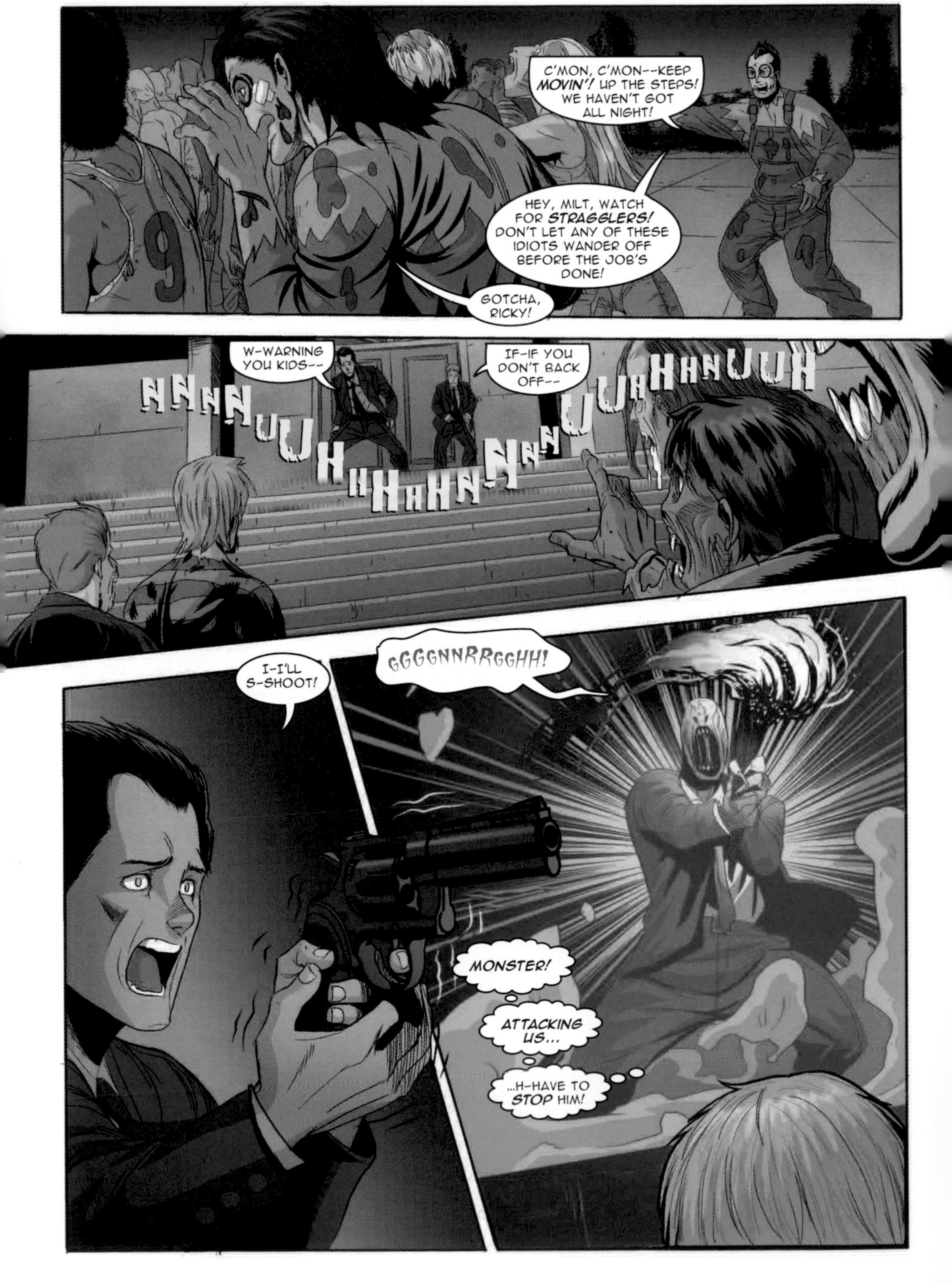

C'MON, C'MON--KEEP MOVIN'! UP THE STEPS! WE HAVEN'T GOT ALL NIGHT!
HEY, MILT, WATCH FOR STRAGGLERS! DON'T LET ANY OF THESE IDIOTS WANDER OFF BEFORE THE JOB'S DONE!
GOTCHA, RICKY!
W-WARNING YOU KIDS--
IF-IF YOU DON'T BACK OFF--
I-I'LL S-SHOOT!
GGGGNNRRGGHH!
MONSTER!
ATTACKING US...
...H-HAVE TO STOP HIM!

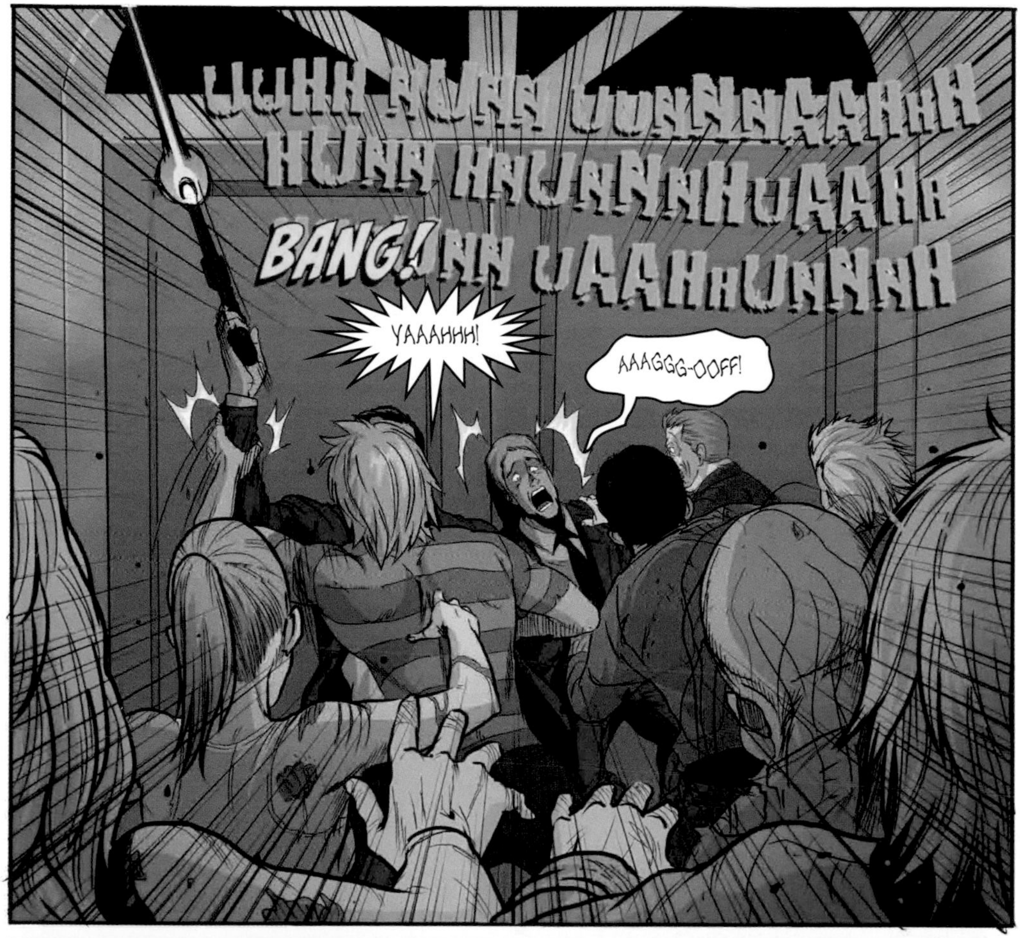
UUHH HUHH UUNNNAAAHHH
HUNH HHUNNNHUAAHH
BANG!
NN UAAHHUNNNH
YAAAHHH!
AAAGGG-OOFF!

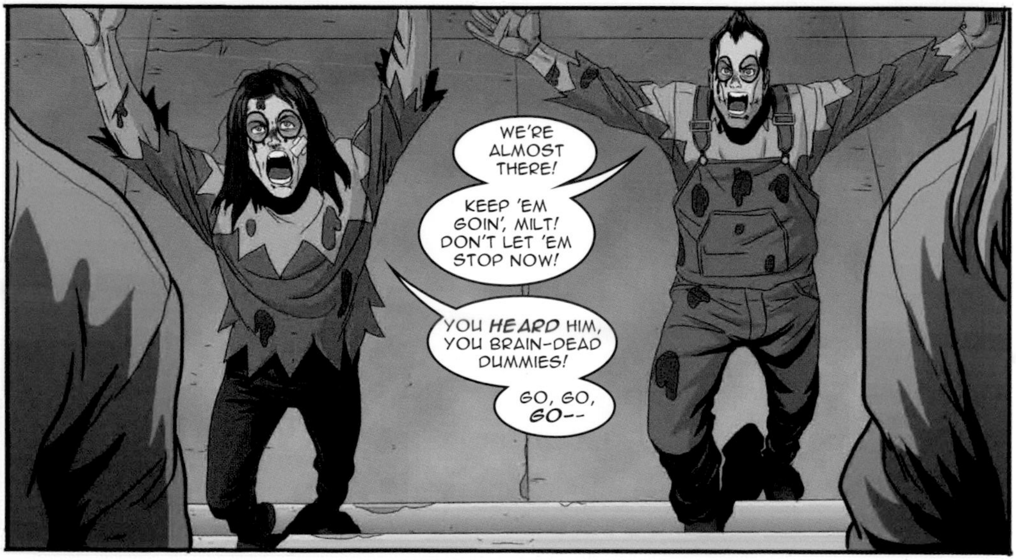
WE'RE ALMOST THERE!
KEEP 'EM GOIN', MILT! DON'T LET 'EM STOP NOW!
YOU HEARD HIM, YOU BRAIN-DEAD DUMMIES!
GO, GO, GO--

CHAPTER SIX: THE MONSTER INSIDE ME

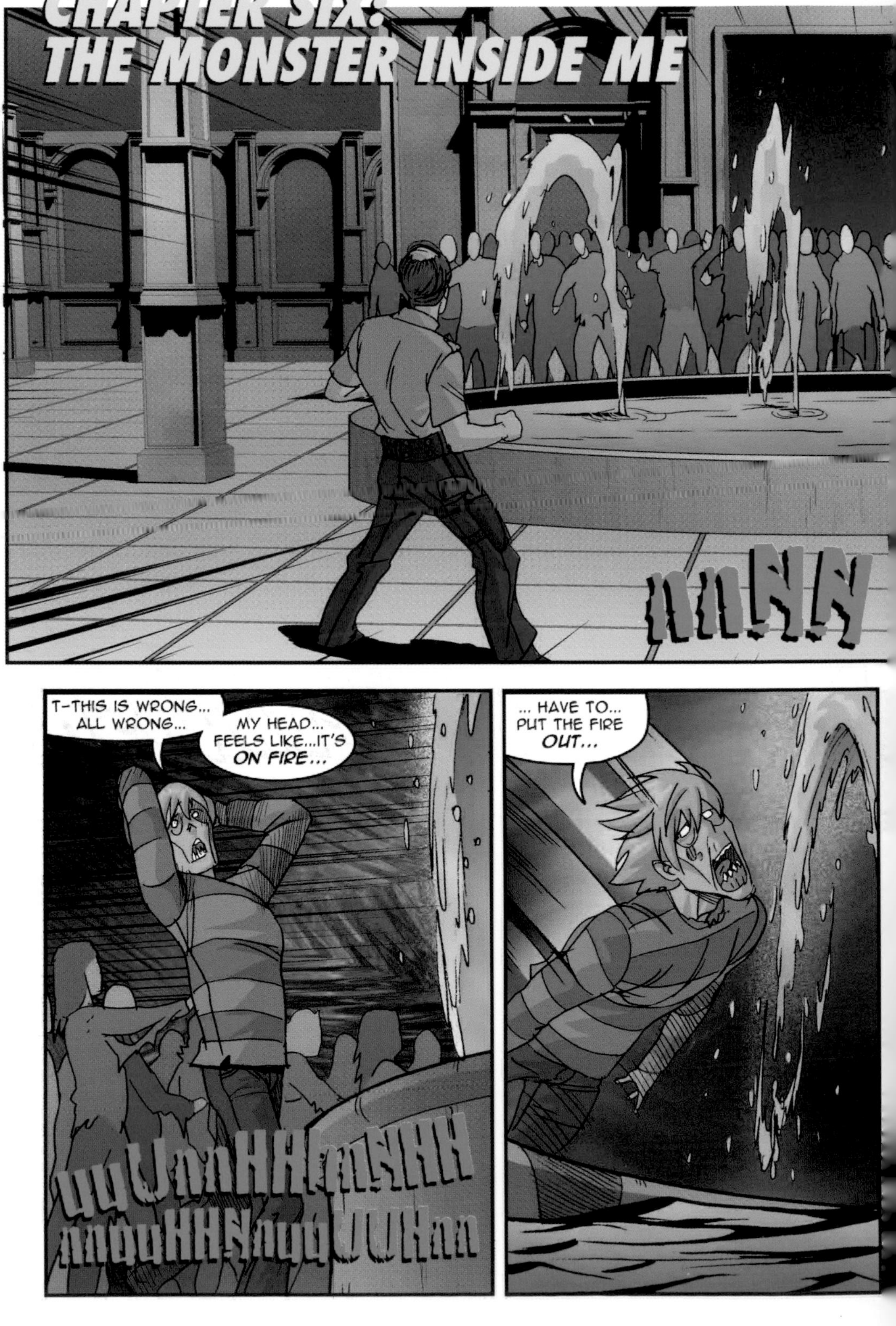
nnNN
T-THIS IS WRONG... ALL WRONG...
MY HEAD... FEELS LIKE...IT'S *ON FIRE...*
uuUnnHHnnNHH
nnguHHNnuuUUHnn
... HAVE TO... PUT THE FIRE *OUT...*

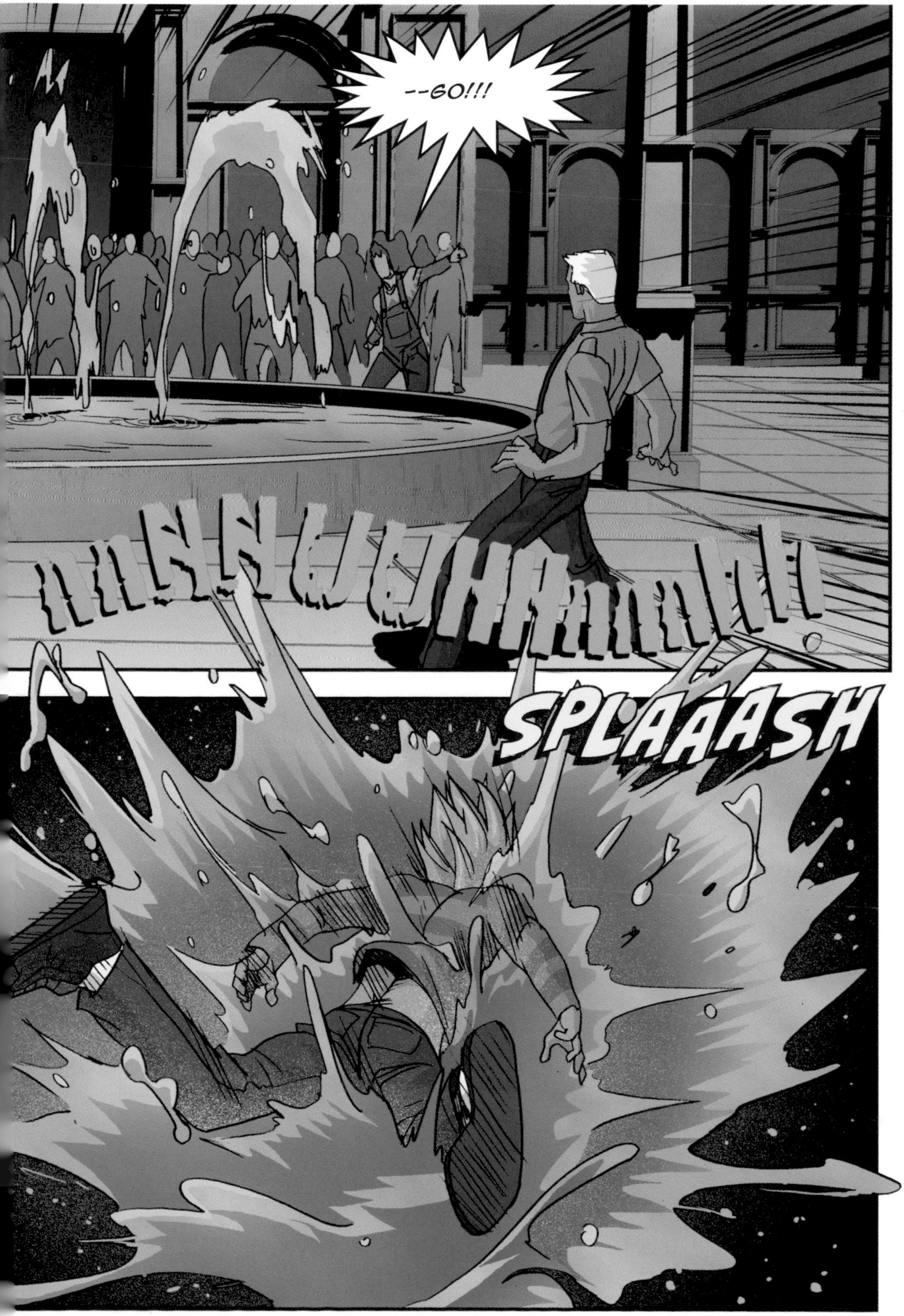
--GO!!!
nnNNUUUHHnnnhh
SPLAAASH

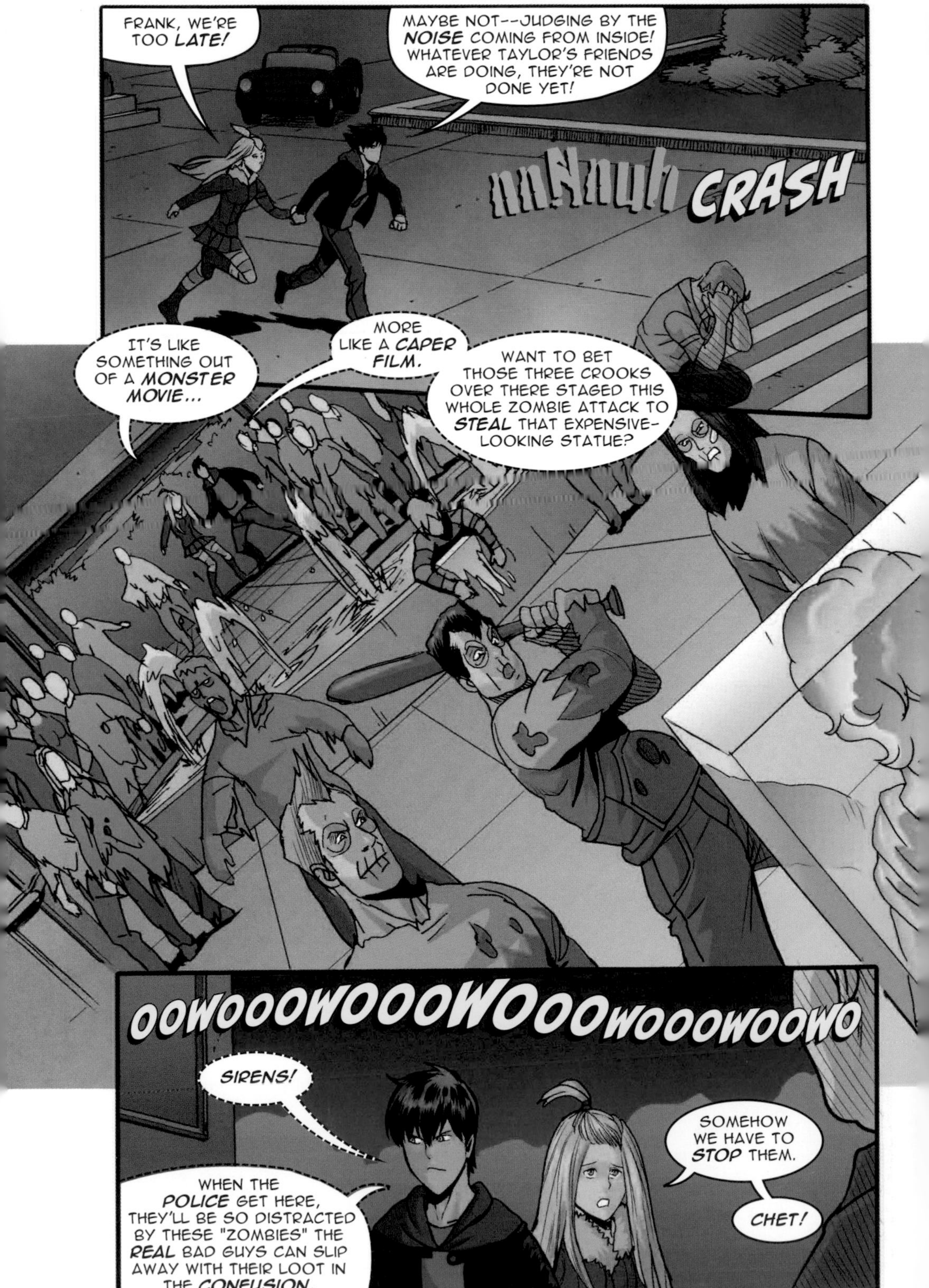

FRANK, WE'RE TOO LATE!
MAYBE NOT--JUDGING BY THE NOISE COMING FROM INSIDE! WHATEVER TAYLOR'S FRIENDS ARE DOING, THEY'RE NOT DONE YET!
nnNnuh
CRASH
IT'S LIKE SOMETHING OUT OF A MONSTER MOVIE...
MORE LIKE A CAPER FILM.
WANT TO BET THOSE THREE CROOKS OVER THERE STAGED THIS WHOLE ZOMBIE ATTACK TO STEAL THAT EXPENSIVE-LOOKING STATUE?
OOWOOOWOOOWOOOWOOOWOOOWOOWO
SIRENS!
WHEN THE POLICE GET HERE, THEY'LL BE SO DISTRACTED BY THESE "ZOMBIES" THE REAL BAD GUYS CAN SLIP AWAY WITH THEIR LOOT IN THE CONFUSION.
SOMEHOW WE HAVE TO STOP THEM.
CHET!

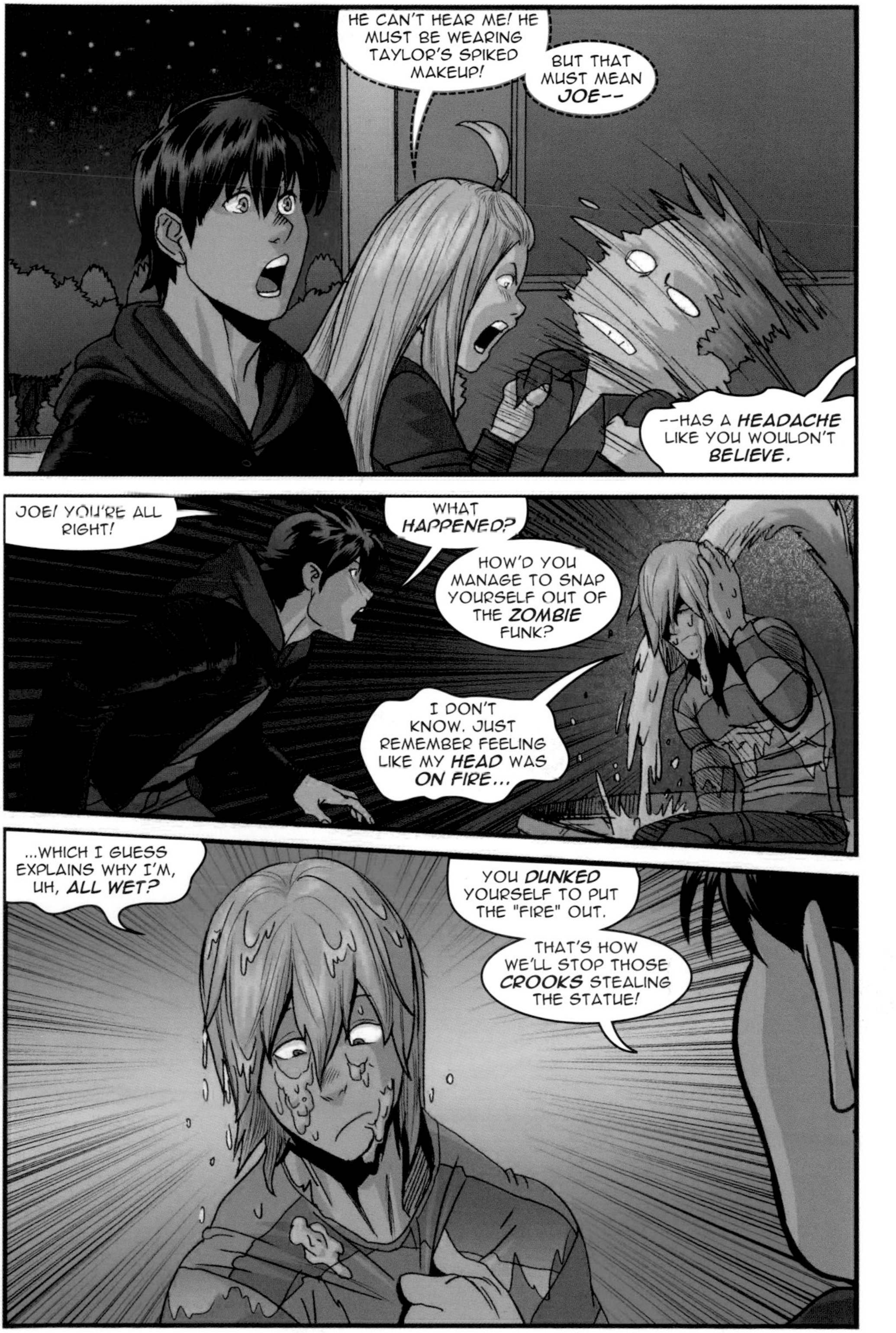
HE CAN'T HEAR ME! HE MUST BE WEARING TAYLOR'S SPIKED MAKEUP!
BUT THAT MUST MEAN JOE--
--HAS A HEADACHE LIKE YOU WOULDN'T BELIEVE.
JOE! YOU'RE ALL RIGHT!
WHAT HAPPENED?
HOW'D YOU MANAGE TO SNAP YOURSELF OUT OF THE ZOMBIE FUNK?
I DON'T KNOW. JUST REMEMBER FEELING LIKE MY HEAD WAS ON FIRE...
...WHICH I GUESS EXPLAINS WHY I'M, UH, ALL WET?
YOU DUNKED YOURSELF TO PUT THE "FIRE" OUT.
THAT'S HOW WE'LL STOP THOSE CROOKS STEALING THE STATUE!

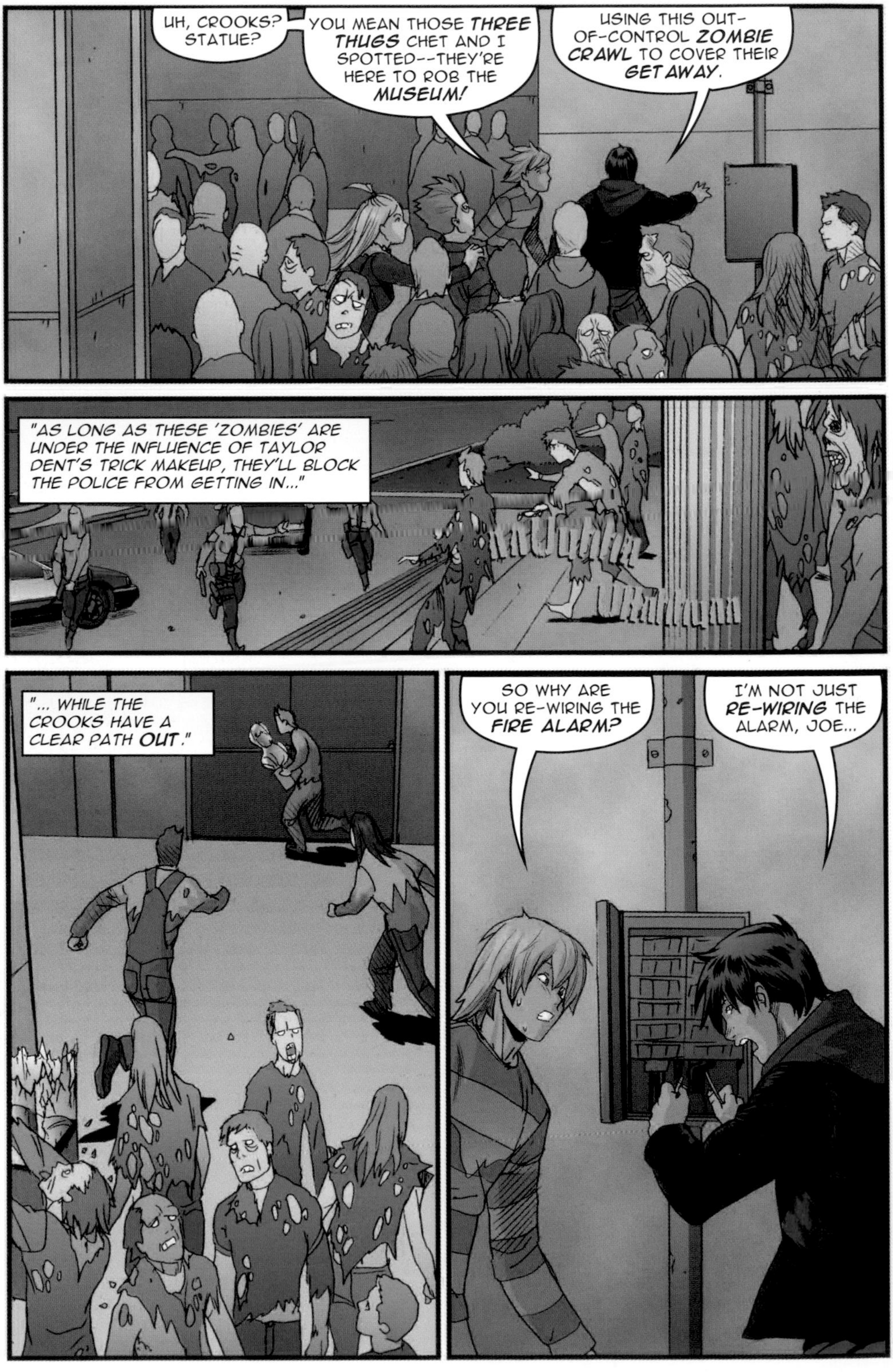
UH, CROOKS? STATUE?
YOU MEAN THOSE THREE THUGS CHET AND I SPOTTED--THEY'RE HERE TO ROB THE MUSEUM!
USING THIS OUT-OF-CONTROL ZOMBIE CRAWL TO COVER THEIR GETAWAY.
"AS LONG AS THESE 'ZOMBIES' ARE UNDER THE INFLUENCE OF TAYLOR DENT'S TRICK MAKEUP, THEY'LL BLOCK THE POLICE FROM GETTING IN..."
"... WHILE THE CROOKS HAVE A CLEAR PATH OUT."
SO WHY ARE YOU RE-WIRING THE FIRE ALARM?
I'M NOT JUST RE-WIRING THE ALARM, JOE...

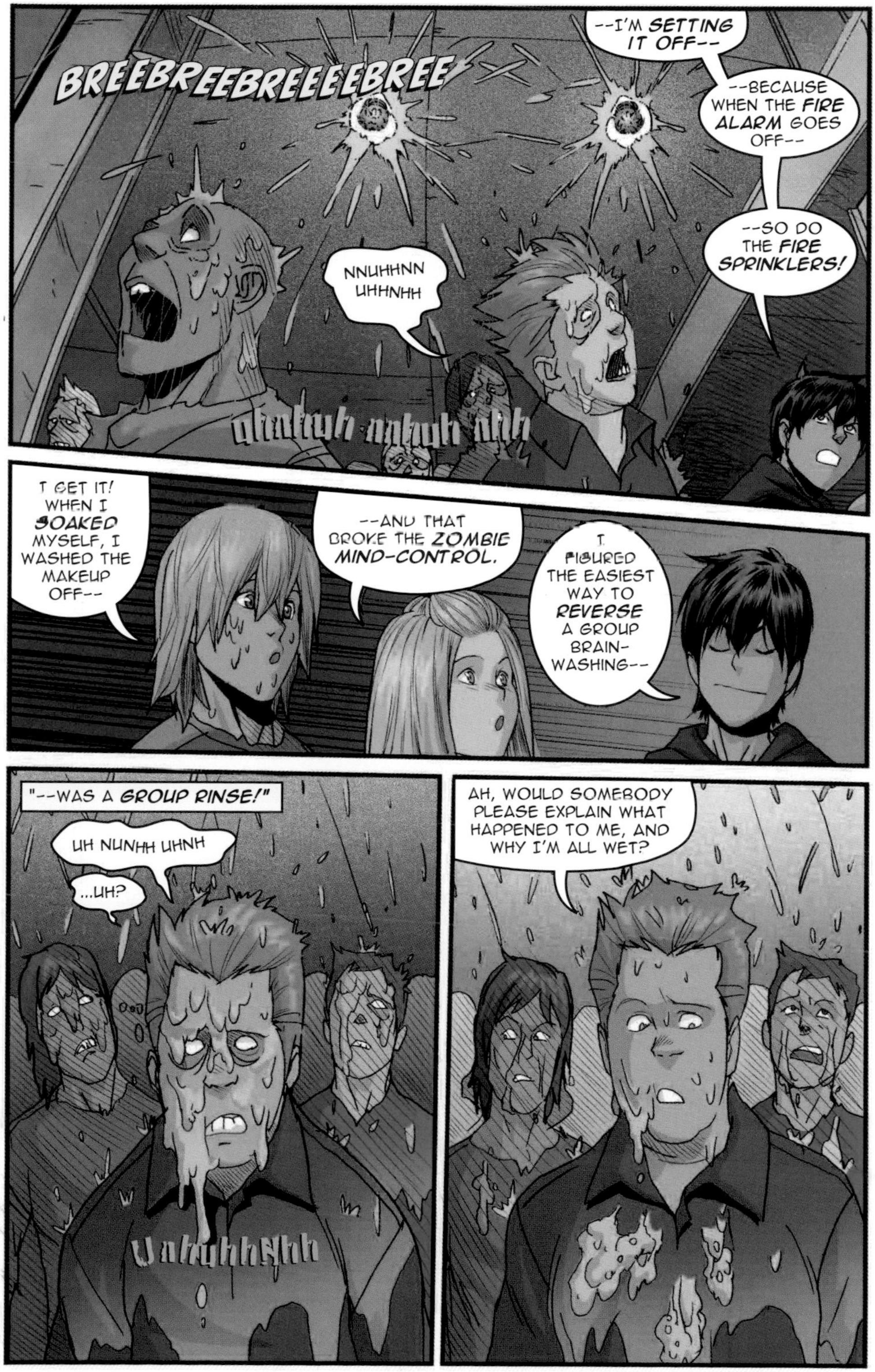
BREEBREEBREEEEEBREE
--I'M SETTING IT OFF--
--BECAUSE WHEN THE FIRE ALARM GOES OFF--
--SO DO THE FIRE SPRINKLERS!
NNUHHNN UHHNHH
I GET IT! WHEN I SOAKED MYSELF, I WASHED THE MAKEUP OFF--
--AND THAT BROKE THE ZOMBIE MIND-CONTROL.
I FIGURED THE EASIEST WAY TO REVERSE A GROUP BRAIN-WASHING--
"--WAS A GROUP RINSE!"
UH NUNHH UHNH
...UH?
AH, WOULD SOMEBODY PLEASE EXPLAIN WHAT HAPPENED TO ME, AND WHY I'M ALL WET?

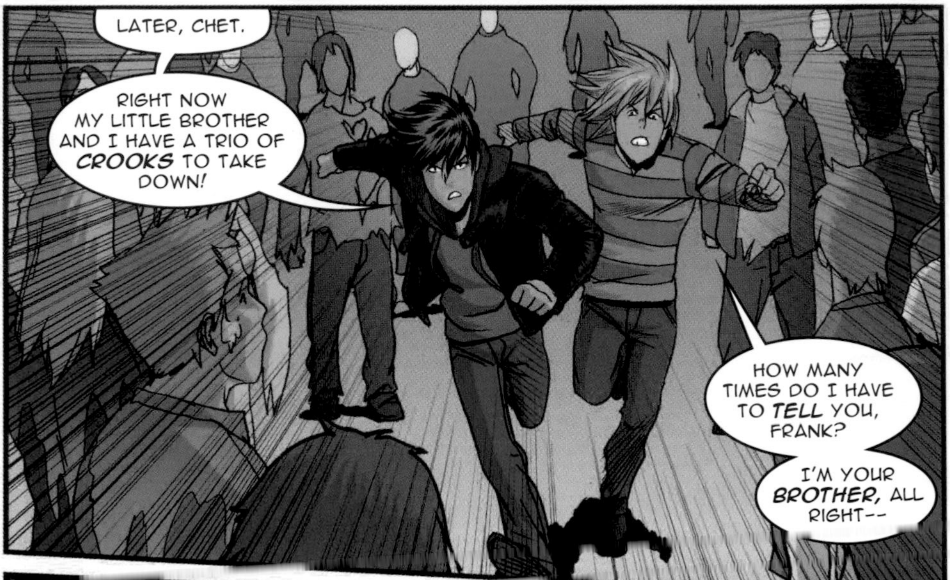
LATER, CHET.
RIGHT NOW MY LITTLE BROTHER AND I HAVE A TRIO OF **CROOKS** TO TAKE DOWN!
HOW MANY TIMES DO I HAVE TO **TELL** YOU, FRANK?
I'M YOUR **BROTHER,** ALL RIGHT--

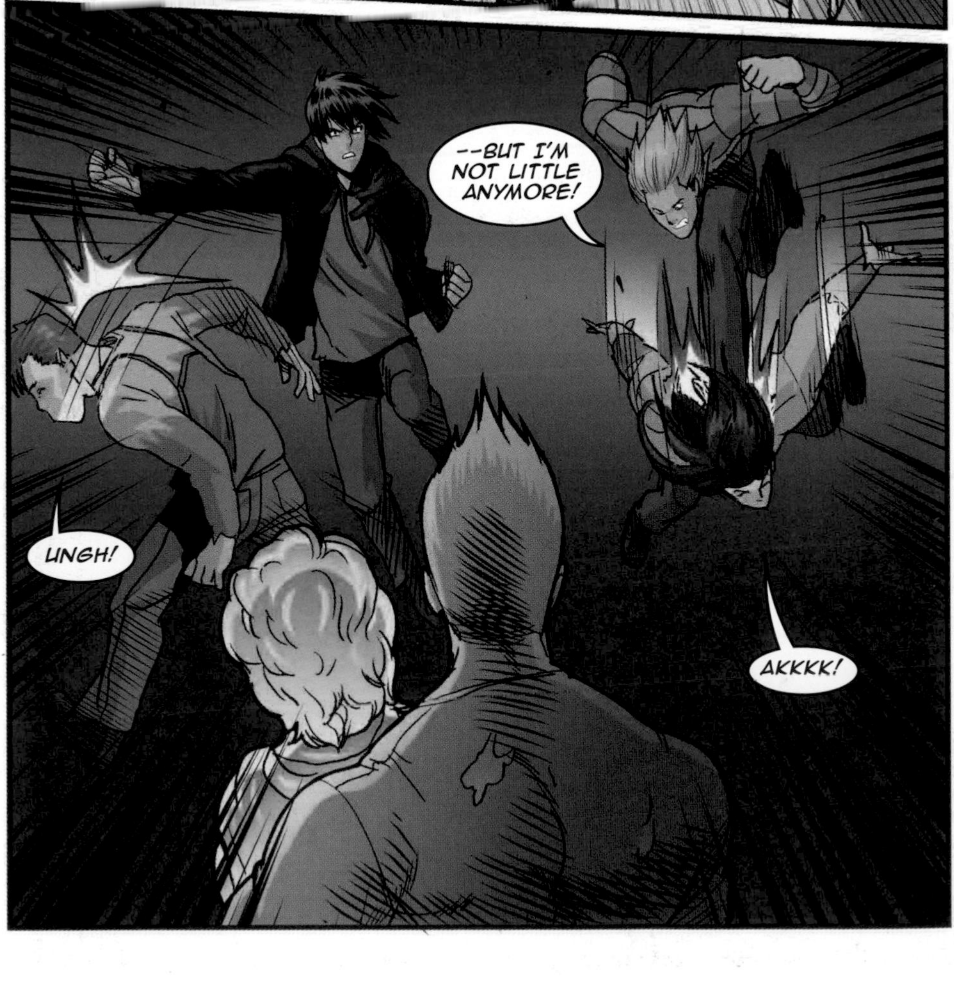
--BUT I'M NOT LITTLE ANYMORE!
UNGH!
AKKKK!

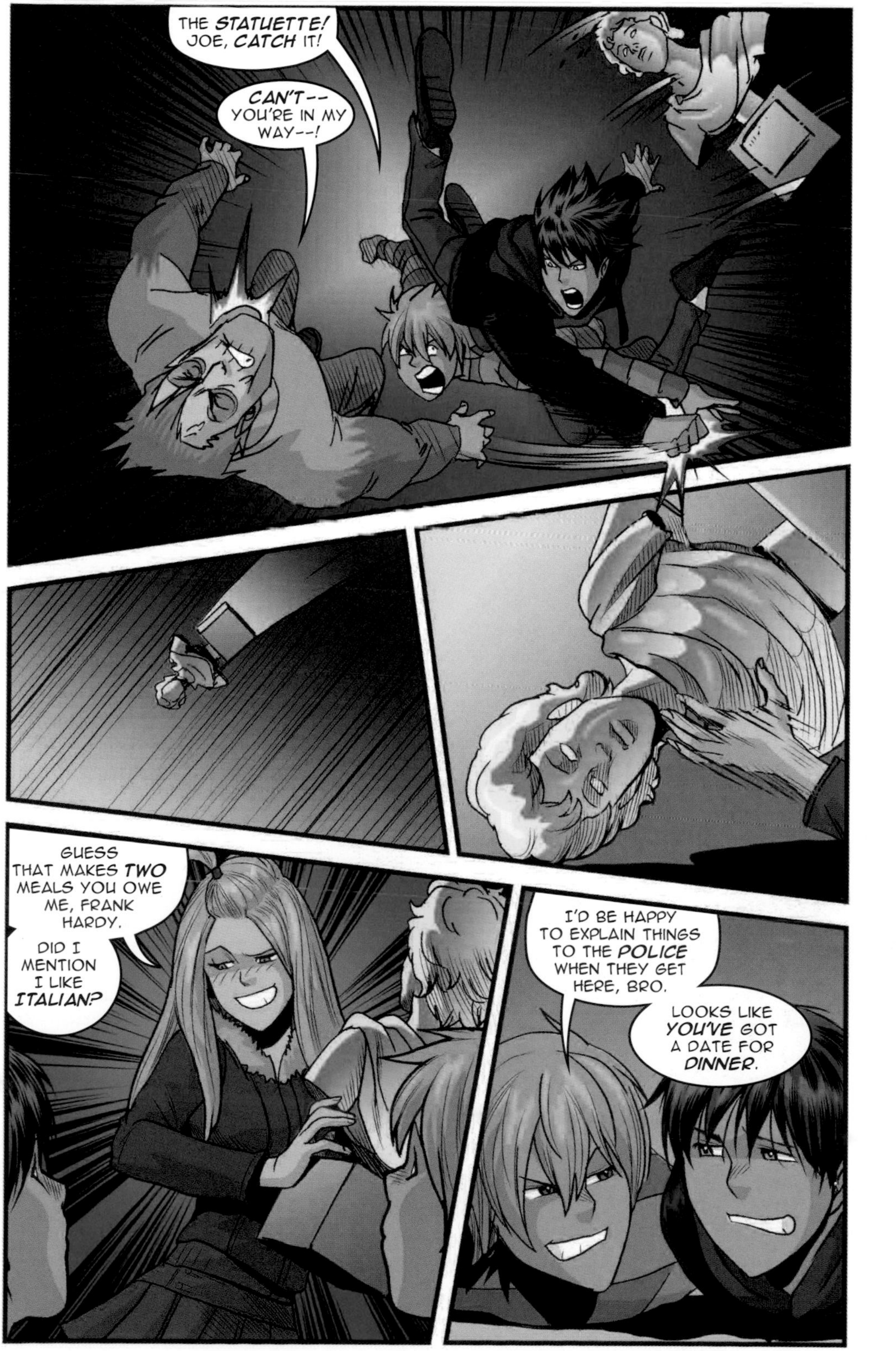
THE STATUETTE! JOE, CATCH IT!
CAN'T-- YOU'RE IN MY WAY--!
GUESS THAT MAKES TWO MEALS YOU OWE ME, FRANK HARDY.
DID I MENTION I LIKE ITALIAN?
I'D BE HAPPY TO EXPLAIN THINGS TO THE POLICE WHEN THEY GET HERE, BRO.
LOOKS LIKE YOU'VE GOT A DATE FOR DINNER.

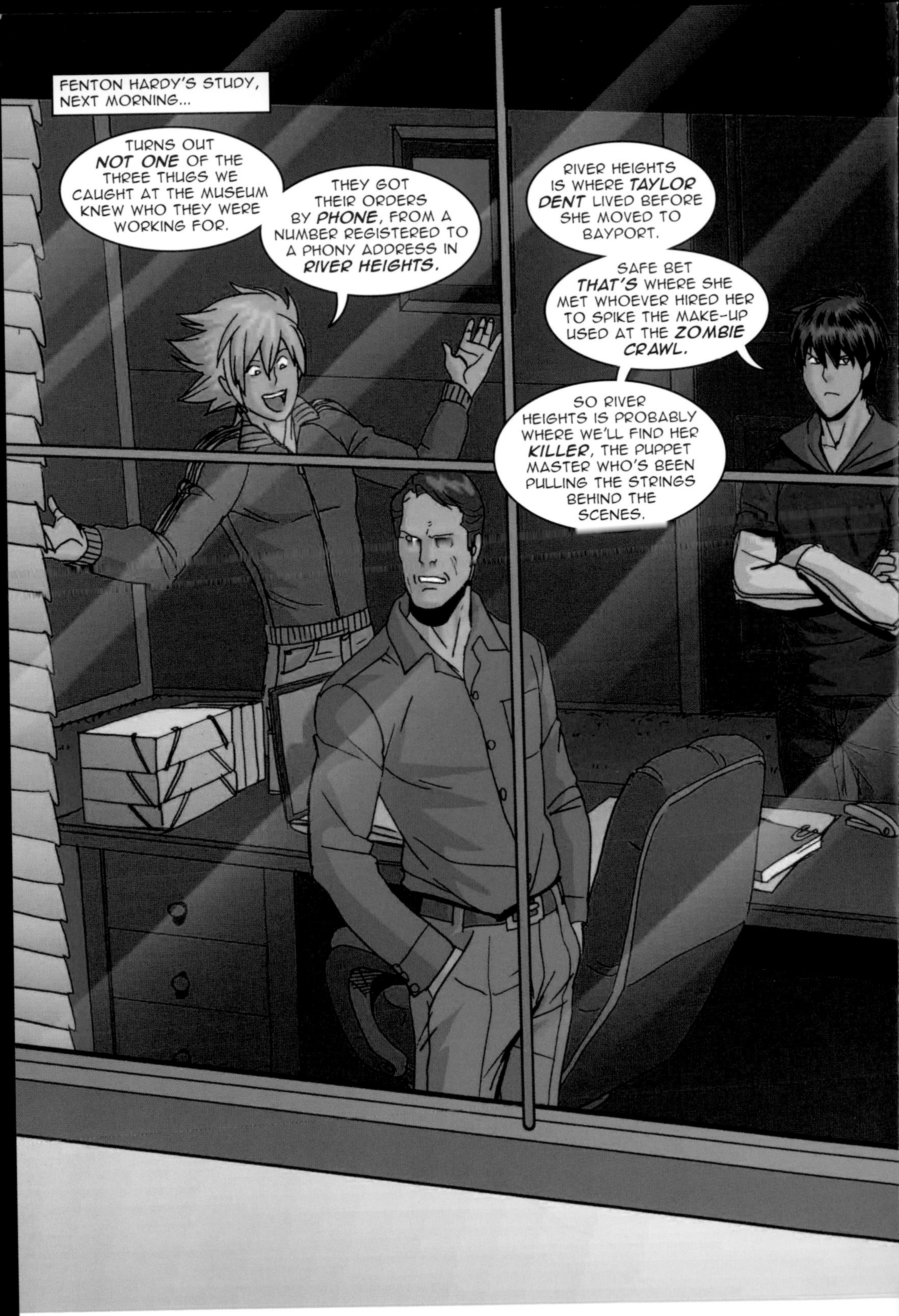
FENTON HARDY'S STUDY, NEXT MORNING...
TURNS OUT NOT ONE OF THE THREE THUGS WE CAUGHT AT THE MUSEUM KNEW WHO THEY WERE WORKING FOR.
THEY GOT THEIR ORDERS BY PHONE, FROM A NUMBER REGISTERED TO A PHONY ADDRESS IN RIVER HEIGHTS.
RIVER HEIGHTS IS WHERE TAYLOR DENT LIVED BEFORE SHE MOVED TO BAYPORT.
SAFE BET THAT'S WHERE SHE MET WHOEVER HIRED HER TO SPIKE THE MAKE-UP USED AT THE ZOMBIE CRAWL.
SO RIVER HEIGHTS IS PROBABLY WHERE WE'LL FIND HER KILLER, THE PUPPET MASTER WHO'S BEEN PULLING THE STRINGS BEHIND THE SCENES.

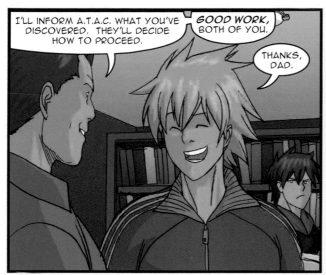

I'LL INFORM A.T.A.C. WHAT YOU'VE DISCOVERED. THEY'LL DECIDE HOW TO PROCEED.

GOOD WORK, BOTH OF YOU.

THANKS, DAD.

FRANK, I KNOW YOU AND JOE HAD *DIFFERENT POINTS OF VIEW* ABOUT HOW TO APPROACH THIS MISSION--

I GUESS THAT'S *ONE* WAY TO LOOK AT IT.

HOW WOULD *YOU* LOOK AT IT, BIG BROTHER?

YOU WENT OFF HALF-COCKED, *WITHOUT* A PLAN, AND ALMOST GOT YOURSELF AND CHET *KILLED.*

BUT WE *WEREN'T* KILLED, AND IF I HADN'T BEEN THERE, AND JUMPED IN THAT *FOUNTAIN,* YOU WOULDN'T HAVE FIGURED OUT HOW TO *STOP* THE CROOKS' GETAWAY.

YOU TOOK A *DUMB RISK,* JOE.

IT WAS A *CALCULATED* RISK, AND I'D DO IT AGAIN.

NOT IF I HAVE ANYTHING TO SAY ABOUT IT.

YOU *WON'T.*

YOU'RE MY *BROTHER,* NOT MY BOSS.

WHAT YOU ARE, IS A *TEAM.* BROTHERS *AND* PARTNERS.

YOU'RE ALSO *BOTH* ABOUT TO BE LATE FOR *SCHOOL.*

DAD'S RIGHT. WE CAN TALK ABOUT THIS *LATER.*

HI, MOM.

BYE, MOM.

FRANK, JOE...

DID I HEAR THE BOYS *ARGUING* ABOUT SOMETHING? IS ANYTHING *WRONG?*

OUR SONS HAVE BEEN "THE HARDY BOYS" SO LONG SOMETIMES WE FORGET THEY'RE *TWO DIFFERENT YOUNG MEN,* WITH THEIR OWN MINDS, AND THEIR OWN *POINTS OF VIEW.*

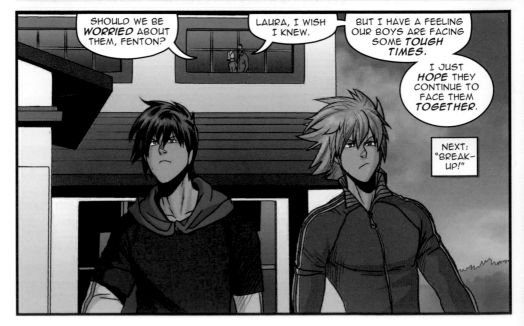

SHOULD WE BE *WORRIED* ABOUT THEM, FENTON?

LAURA, I WISH I KNEW.

BUT I HAVE A FEELING OUR BOYS ARE FACING SOME *TOUGH TIMES.*

I JUST *HOPE* THEY CONTINUE TO FACE THEM *TOGETHER.*

NEXT: "BREAK-UP!"

WATCH OUT FOR PAPERCUTZ™

Welcome to the premiere edition of the all-new THE HARDY BOYS The New Case Files graphic novel series! I'm Jim Salicrup, Editor-in-Chief of Papercutz, publisher of graphic novels for all-ages. If you were a follower of The Hardy Boy's first graphic novel series, welcome back! If you're new to The Hardy Boys in comics form, well, you're in for a wild ride! THE HARDY BOYS is just as action-packed and exciting in comics form as they are in their prose series.

In fact, we strive to preserve all the things that have made The Hardy Boys so popular and successful in their book series in our all-new graphic novel stories. To that end we've enlisted Gerry Conway to write THE HARDY BOYS The New Case Files. Gerry is a legendary comics writer, responsible for some of the most unforgettable comics ever published. Taking over *The Amazing Spider-Man* comic after co-creator Stan Lee left the series, Gerry shocked a generation of Spidey-fans when he killed-off Peter Parker's then true love, Gwen Stacy. Gerry quickly followed that up with Spidey's brutal battle with the Green Goblin. Even if you didn't read the comics, you probably saw it brought to dramatic life on the big screen in the very first blockbuster *Spider-Man* movie. If that wasn't enough, Gerry also created The Punisher, who has also inspired several movie adaptations as well. I could go on and on about Gerry's countless comicbook accomplishments, but then we wouldn't have enough room for any comics in this graphic novel. I will mention though, that back when I was editing the *Spider-Man* titles for Marvel, it was a dream come true to work with Mr. Conway. He understands what makes for exciting, emotionally powerful comics better than anyone—so you can imagine how thrilled we are at Papercutz to have Gerry writing the new adventures of Frank and Joe Hardy. And just as he forever shook up the very foundations of poor Peter Parker's world —expect Gerry to do the same with The Hardy Boys starting right now! Whatever you do, don't miss THE HARDY BOYS The New Case Files #2—the title truly says it all: "Break-Up!"

And speaking of titles, you won't want to miss the premiere of NANCY DREW The New Case Files #1 "Vampire Slayer" Part One. If you're the macho type who thinks that Nancy's graphic novel exploits may be "too girly" for you, you have to see what happens when Nancy meets Gregor Coffin. Is he man or vampire?! We guarantee you never saw a Nancy Drew story like this one before! And if that wasn't enough of a reason, let me mention what sharp-eyed Hardy Boys fans probably already discovered a few pages back—that Taylor Dent is from Nancy Drew's hometown of River Heights. Something strange sure is going on around here—or should I say, over there! Just to give you a little taste of what we're talking about regarding America's favorite Girl Detective we're offering a special preview of NANCY DREW The New Case Files #1 "Vampire Slayer" on the pages following! Check out this small sample, written by Stefan Petrucha and Sarah Kinney, and drawn by Sho Murase, and see if you can resist picking up your own copies of the complete 2-part epic!

That's it for now, but please take a moment to tell us what YOU think of THE HARDY BOYS The New Case Files #1. Either email me at salicrup@papercutz.com or send a letter to The Hardy Boys, c/o PAPERCUTZ, 40 Exchange Place, Suite 1308, New York, NY 10005. We hope to present some of the most interesting comments in our very next volume! Till then, watch out for Papercutz!

Thanks,

Jim

Special preview of NANCY DREW The New Case Files #1 "Vampire Slayer" Part One!

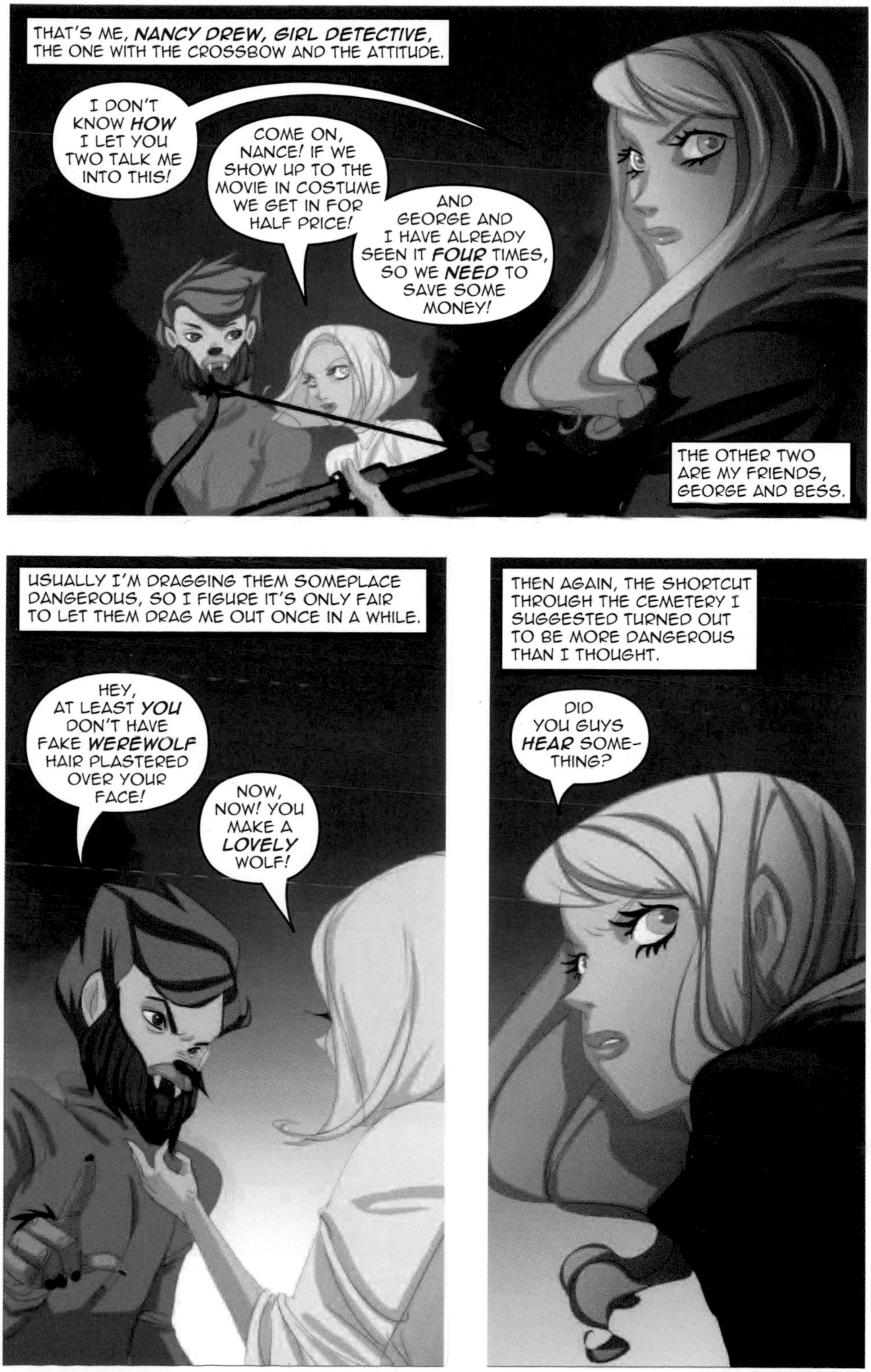
THAT'S ME, NANCY DREW, GIRL DETECTIVE, THE ONE WITH THE CROSSBOW AND THE ATTITUDE.
I DON'T KNOW HOW I LET YOU TWO TALK ME INTO THIS!
COME ON, NANCE! IF WE SHOW UP TO THE MOVIE IN COSTUME WE GET IN FOR HALF PRICE!
AND GEORGE AND I HAVE ALREADY SEEN IT FOUR TIMES, SO WE NEED TO SAVE SOME MONEY!
THE OTHER TWO ARE MY FRIENDS, GEORGE AND BESS.
USUALLY I'M DRAGGING THEM SOMEPLACE DANGEROUS, SO I FIGURE IT'S ONLY FAIR TO LET THEM DRAG ME OUT ONCE IN A WHILE.
HEY, AT LEAST YOU DON'T HAVE FAKE WEREWOLF HAIR PLASTERED OVER YOUR FACE!
NOW, NOW! YOU MAKE A LOVELY WOLF!
THEN AGAIN, THE SHORTCUT THROUGH THE CEMETERY I SUGGESTED TURNED OUT TO BE MORE DANGEROUS THAN I THOUGHT.
DID YOU GUYS HEAR SOME-THING?

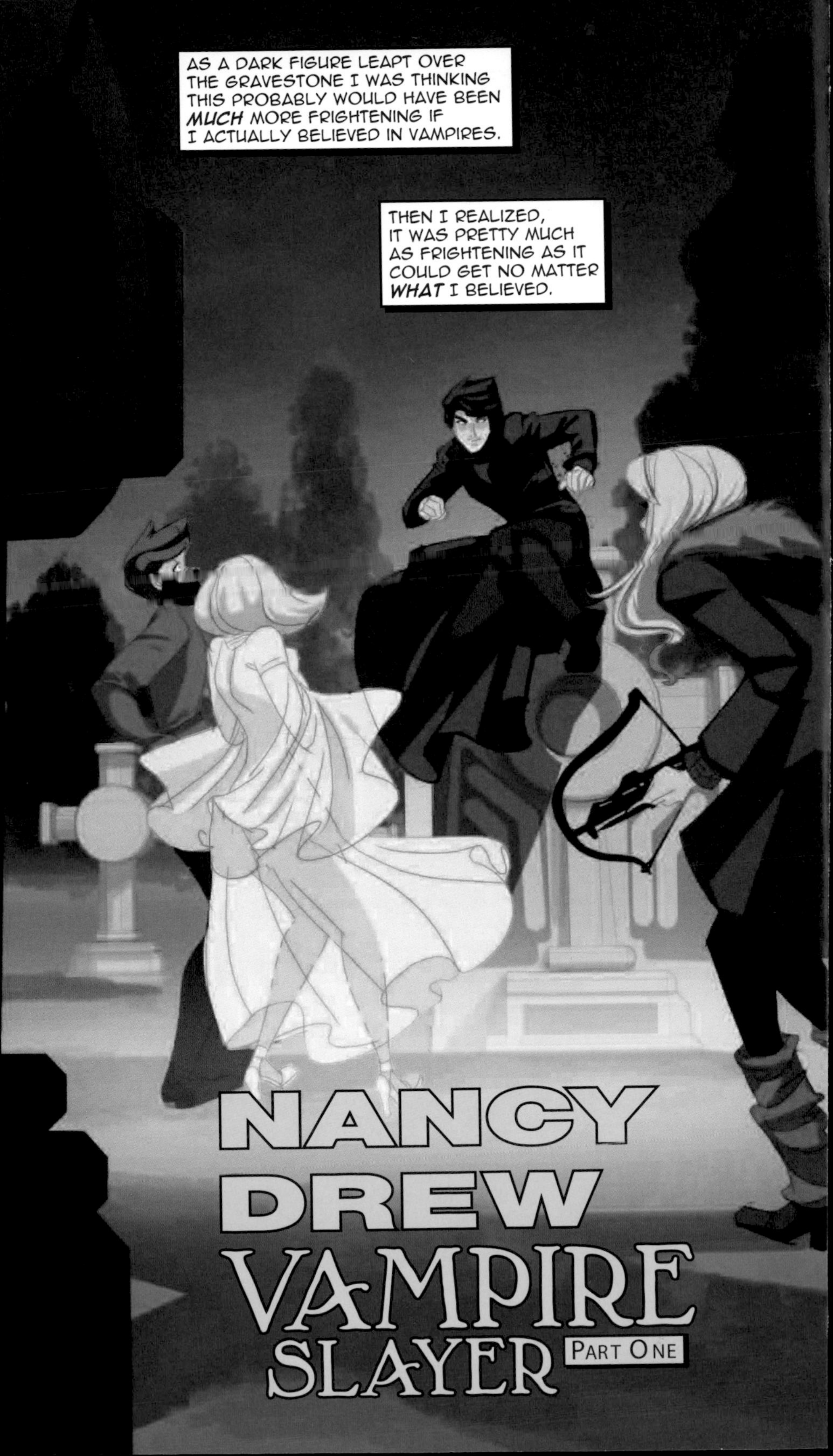
AS A DARK FIGURE LEAPT OVER THE GRAVESTONE I WAS THINKING THIS PROBABLY WOULD HAVE BEEN *MUCH* MORE FRIGHTENING IF I ACTUALLY BELIEVED IN VAMPIRES.
THEN I REALIZED, IT WAS PRETTY MUCH AS FRIGHTENING AS IT COULD GET NO MATTER *WHAT* I BELIEVED.
NANCY DREW
VAMPIRE SLAYER
PART ONE

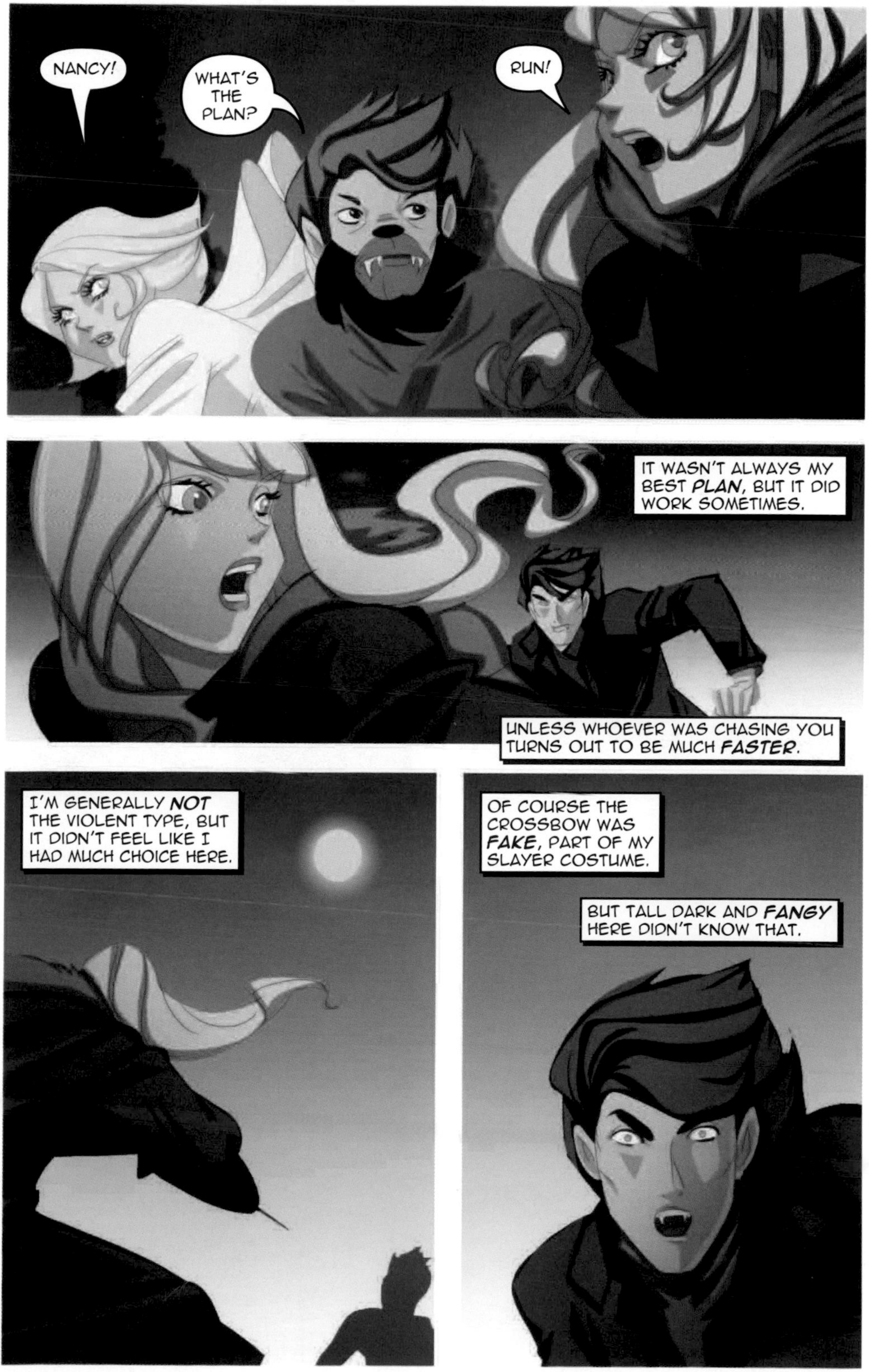
NANCY!
WHAT'S THE PLAN?
RUN!
IT WASN'T ALWAYS MY BEST PLAN, BUT IT DID WORK SOMETIMES.
UNLESS WHOEVER WAS CHASING YOU TURNS OUT TO BE MUCH FASTER.
I'M GENERALLY NOT THE VIOLENT TYPE, BUT IT DIDN'T FEEL LIKE I HAD MUCH CHOICE HERE.
OF COURSE THE CROSSBOW WAS FAKE, PART OF MY SLAYER COSTUME.
BUT TALL DARK AND FANGY HERE DIDN'T KNOW THAT.

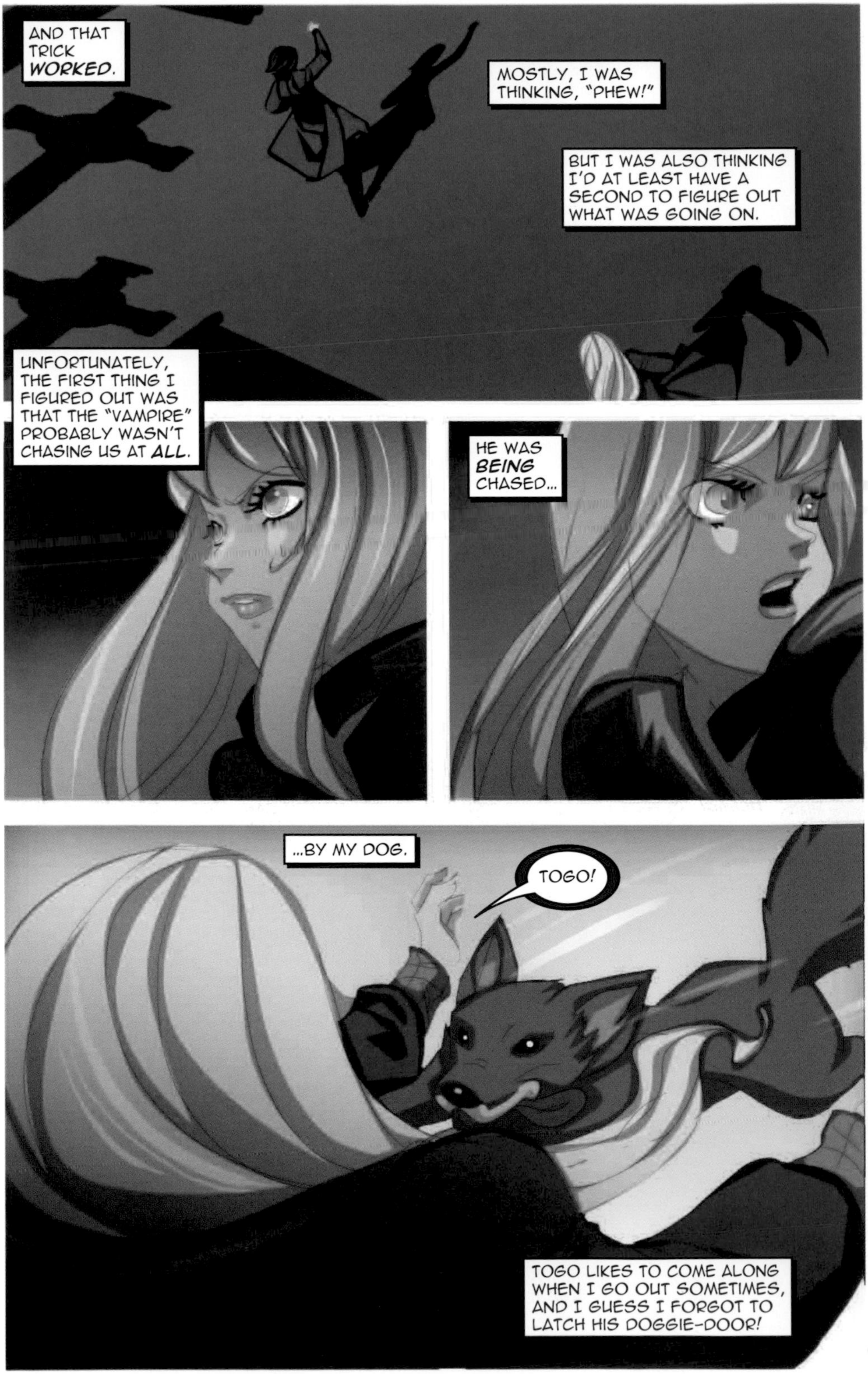
AND THAT TRICK WORKED.
MOSTLY, I WAS THINKING, "PHEW!"
BUT I WAS ALSO THINKING I'D AT LEAST HAVE A SECOND TO FIGURE OUT WHAT WAS GOING ON.
UNFORTUNATELY, THE FIRST THING I FIGURED OUT WAS THAT THE "VAMPIRE" PROBABLY WASN'T CHASING US AT ALL.
HE WAS BEING CHASED...
...BY MY DOG.
TOGO!
TOGO LIKES TO COME ALONG WHEN I GO OUT SOMETIMES, AND I GUESS I FORGOT TO LATCH HIS DOGGIE-DOOR!

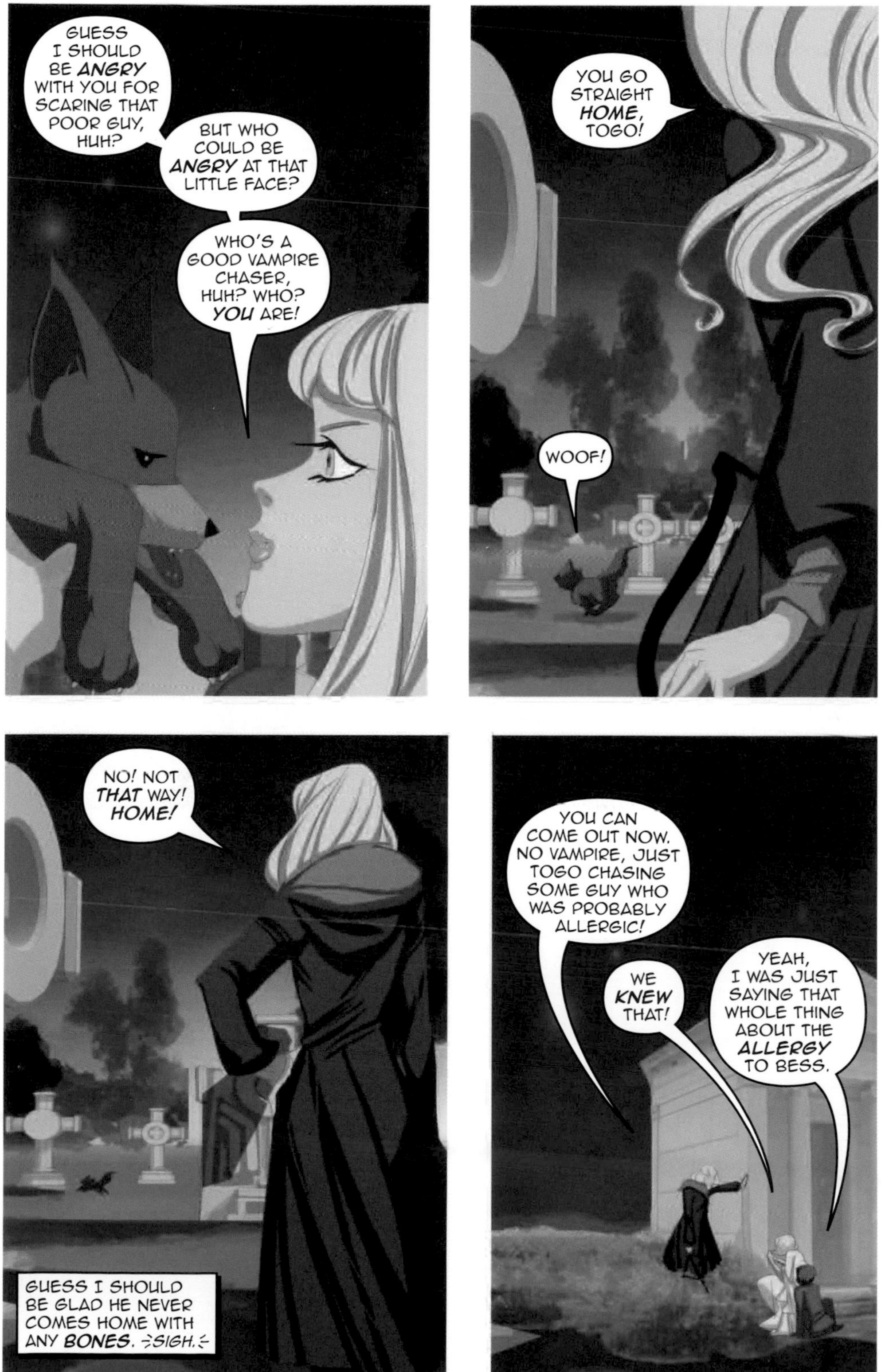
GUESS I SHOULD BE ANGRY WITH YOU FOR SCARING THAT POOR GUY, HUH?
BUT WHO COULD BE ANGRY AT THAT LITTLE FACE?
WHO'S A GOOD VAMPIRE CHASER, HUH? WHO? YOU ARE!
YOU GO STRAIGHT HOME, TOGO!
WOOF!
NO! NOT THAT WAY! HOME!
GUESS I SHOULD BE GLAD HE NEVER COMES HOME WITH ANY BONES. *SIGH.*
YOU CAN COME OUT NOW. NO VAMPIRE, JUST TOGO CHASING SOME GUY WHO WAS PROBABLY ALLERGIC!
WE KNEW THAT!
YEAH, I WAS JUST SAYING THAT WHOLE THING ABOUT THE ALLERGY TO BESS.

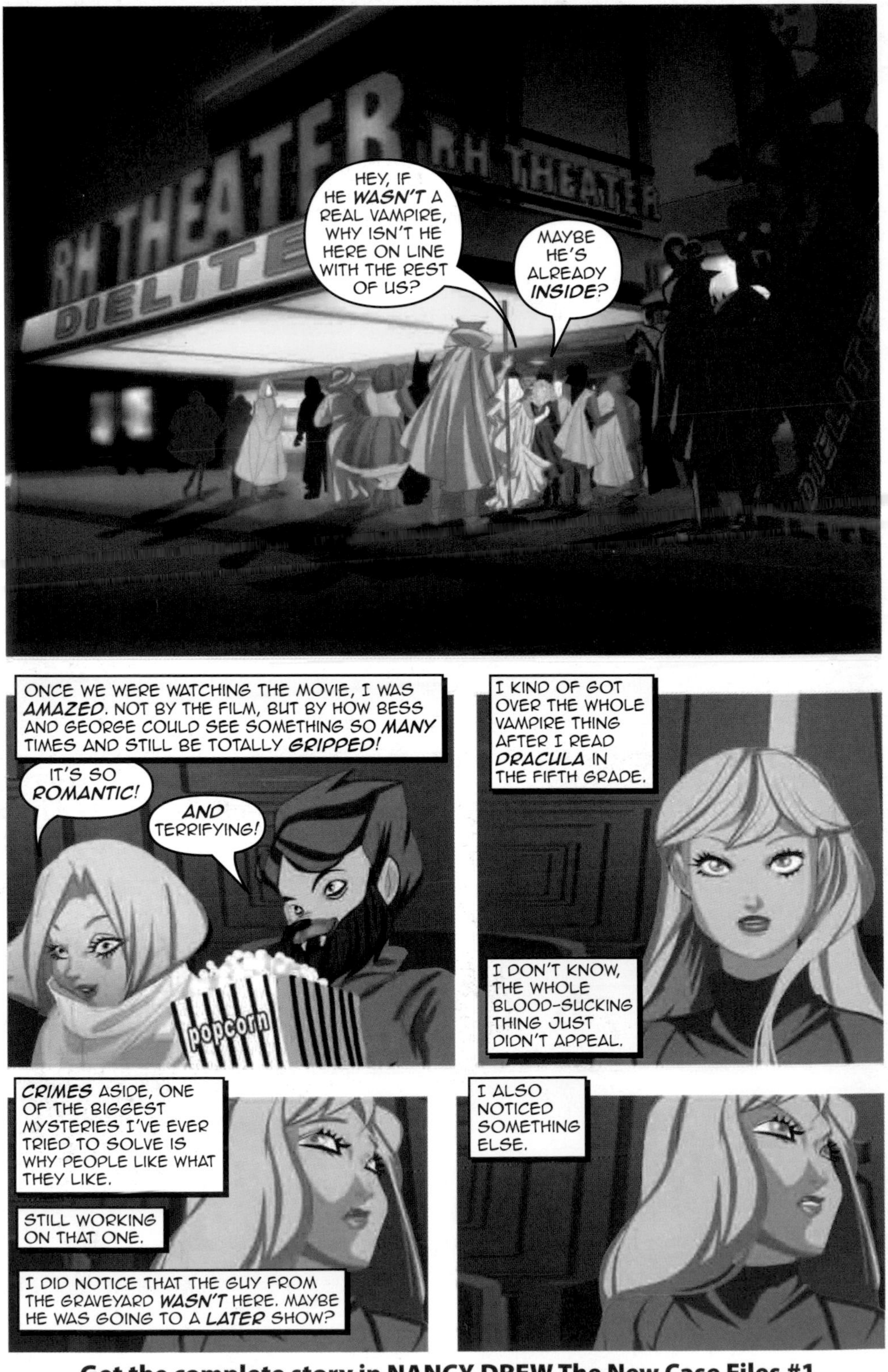
RH THEATER
DIELITE
RH THEATER
HEY, IF HE WASN'T A REAL VAMPIRE, WHY ISN'T HE HERE ON LINE WITH THE REST OF US?
MAYBE HE'S ALREADY INSIDE?
ONCE WE WERE WATCHING THE MOVIE, I WAS AMAZED. NOT BY THE FILM, BUT BY HOW BESS AND GEORGE COULD SEE SOMETHING SO MANY TIMES AND STILL BE TOTALLY GRIPPED!
IT'S SO ROMANTIC!
AND TERRIFYING!
popcorn
I KIND OF GOT OVER THE WHOLE VAMPIRE THING AFTER I READ DRACULA IN THE FIFTH GRADE.
I DON'T KNOW, THE WHOLE BLOOD-SUCKING THING JUST DIDN'T APPEAL.
CRIMES ASIDE, ONE OF THE BIGGEST MYSTERIES I'VE EVER TRIED TO SOLVE IS WHY PEOPLE LIKE WHAT THEY LIKE.
STILL WORKING ON THAT ONE.
I DID NOTICE THAT THE GUY FROM THE GRAVEYARD WASN'T HERE. MAYBE HE WAS GOING TO A LATER SHOW?
I ALSO NOTICED SOMETHING ELSE.

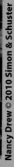

Recover Royal Treasure on the Rails in Europe in

THE HARDY BOYS®
TREASURE ON THE TRACKS